DYING TO WRITE

by
The Write Word Writers

Heddon Publishing

First edition published in 2025 by Heddon Publishing.

Copyright © The Write Word 2025, all rights reserved.

No part of this book may be reproduced, adapted, stored in a retrieval system or transmitted by any means, electronic, photocopying, or otherwise without prior permission of the author.

ISBN 978-1-917824-04-0

Cover artwork by Jane Gill

Images courtesy of

Gill Leese: Chapters 1, 4, 5, 9, 10, 11, 12

Jill Taylor: Chapters 2, 3, 6, 7, 13, 19, 20, 22, epilogue and Writers' Retreat Flier

This is a work of fiction. Names, characters, businesses, places, events and incidents are either the products of the authors' imagination or used in a fictitious manner. Any resemblance to actual persons, living or dead, or actual events is purely coincidental.

www.heddonpublishing.com

www.facebook.com/heddonpublishing

Contributing Authors

Gill Leese, Jilly Taylor, Jenny Birchall, Julie Ann Jones, Helen Dunshea, Anne Renshaw, Ann Glover, Jane Gill and Stella M. Ashbrook.

"All contributing authors retain copyright to their individual contributions, including characters and images, which are used in this compilation with their permission."

The compilation copyright © 2025 by The Write Word

(Jane Gill and Stella M. Ashbrook)

"The Write Word holds the copyright in the selection, arrangement, and presentation of this work as a collective whole."

Cambridge News

Volume 03, Tuesday 10th March 1936 By Ludvig Temple

AN ANCIENT TREASURE UNVEILED: RARE MAYAN MANUSCRIPT AQUIRED BY CAMBRIDGE UNIVERSITY LIBRARY

In an auction of unparalleled significance held in London yesterday, a manuscript of immense historical and scholarly value was acquired by the Cambridge University Library for the sum of £4,750. This rare document, known as the "Mayan Codex," is believed to contain detailed accounts of the lost treasures of an ancient South American civilization, potentially linked to the fabled wealth of the Inca Empire.

The origins of the manuscript are shrouded in mystery. Said to have been discovered in the depths of a private collection in Spain, the document is attributed to a 17th-century Jesuit chronicler who transcribed the oral traditions of the Mayan people, an obscure and little-documented sect believed to have possessed knowledge of hidden riches.

The codex, written in an elaborate hand with faded illustrations, purports to describe caches of gold, silver, and sacred artifacts concealed during the Spanish conquest.

Experts at Cambridge, eager to authenticate the document, have begun an extensive study of its contents. The codex's delicate pages suggest a mixture of indigenous script and early Spanish annotations, pointing to its antiquity. Professor Alfred Pendleton, an esteemed historian at the University, remarked, "If verified, this manuscript could reshape our understanding of pre-Columbian history and the movements of lost treasure hoards."

The acquisition has been met with both excitement and speculation. Treasure hunters and historians alike have long searched for concrete evidence of hidden troves scattered across the Andes, and many wonder whether this manuscript could be the key to unearthing them. Already, whispers of clandestine expeditions are circulating in learned circles, with many eager to test the codex's cryptic clues.

The University has assured that the manuscript will be carefully preserved and made available for scholarly study

Volume 03, Tuesday 12th March 1946

Cambridge News By Ludvig Temple

MYSTERY AT CAMBRIDGE: PRICELESS MANUSCRIPT STOLEN IN DARING HEIST

Authorities Baffled as Mayan Codex Vanishes Without a Trace

A theft of staggering proportions has occurred at the Cambridge University Library, where the famed Mayan Codex, a manuscript of immeasurable historical importance, was stolen in the dead of night. The daring burglary, which took place sometime between Saturday evening and early Sunday morning, has left police and University officials scrambling for answers.

The Codex, which had been locked within the rare manuscripts room under strict security, disappeared without any signs of forced entry. Library staff discovered its absence when conducting routine inspections, sending shockwaves through the academic community. Inspector Reginald Harcourt of the Cambridge Police stated, "There are no indications of a break-in, suggesting that the perpetrator had intimate knowledge of the library's inner workings." The possibility of an inside job has not been ruled out, nor has the theory that foreign agents may have sought the manuscript for its supposed treasure maps and secrets. Speculation has run rampant in the wake of the heist. Was the theft orchestrated by rogue treasure hunters hoping to unlock the codex's secrets? Could it have been a black-market collector seeking to hoard its knowledge? Some whisper that intelligence agencies, in the chaotic aftermath of the war, may have had a hand in its disappearance, though no concrete evidence has emerged.

The loss is a devastating blow to historical scholarship. Professor Alfred Pendleton, visibly shaken, commented, "We were on the verge of groundbreaking discoveries. The Codex contained information that could have rewritten history. Now, it is lost to us—perhaps forever."

Despite exhaustive searches and international alerts, the Mayan Codex remains missing. No ransom demands have been made, no leads have surfaced, and its whereabouts are unknown. Some believe it has been destroyed; others suggest it still exists, hidden in the hands of a secretive collector.

To this day, the fate of the Mayan Codex remains one of the greatest unsolved mysteries of academia. Will it ever resurface? Only time will tell.

RAVENSHADE MANOR

on the outskirts of historic Cambridge

You are invited to
a 5-day all-inclusive

Writers
Retreat

unlock your creative potential

With Workshops hosted by

FREDDIE HUGHES
an inspiring young author
Plus:
JEREMY PENDLETON
Well-known established author

Are you ready to improve your writing skills?
Reconnect with your creative self? or
Are you simply dying to write?

Come and join us in the serene and secluded surroundings of the Stately Ravenshade Manor and find motivation and support with like-minded writers and knowledgeable Tutors. Giving you time and space to write, free from every-day distractions.

- Fully catered
- Daily writing workshops
- Access to stunning grounds to take a stroll and gain inspiration
- Evening readings and feedback sessions

- Comfortable communal writing room
- Plenty of writing resources and a beautiful library
- Acquire the skills you need to become a confident writer

For further details and to book please contact:
GINA MEREDITH – e-mail: gina@ravenshadeevents.co.uk

PROLOGUE

Cambridge, 1946

Rain tapped gently on the arched windows of the University Library, a quiet rhythm against the hush of the late hour. Most of the building had long since emptied, students retiring to their rooms, lecturers heading to the pubs, but in the far recesses of the Rare Manuscripts Room, a man stood with gloved hands and a heart pounding far too loudly for a scholar.

Alfred Pendleton was not supposed to be there.

It lay before him on the reading table, its leather cover cracked with time, ancient glyphs pressed deep into its spine. The Mayan Codex: a priceless relic of the pre-Columbian world, untranslatable, its purpose unknown, except to him. To the right kind of mind, this was not just a manuscript. It was a map, a secret; a legacy waiting to be rewritten and treasure to be found.

He glanced once over his shoulder. Silence.

With practised ease, he slid the Codex into a satchel, replacing it with a decoy bound in similar hide. He extinguished the lamp, leaving the room cloaked in shadow.

No one saw him leave.

The writing retreat was a rare opportunity to spend five days with rising literary star Freddie Hughes and the faded crime writer Jeremy Pendleton in the Georgian splendour of Ravenshade Manor. A chance to learn from the masters themselves, and perhaps to discover why Jeremy's skill, and reputation, had faded since his glory days of writing over 30 years ago.

For most, it was the opportunity of a lifetime. For one, it was the perfect cover.

The manor loomed on the swoop of the drive, its stone gates topped with ravens and the sweeping drive lined with oak trees, wrapped in ivy and time, its crooked chimneys coughing smoke into the early autumn air. Behind oak doors carved with the Ravenshade crest awaited secrets soaked in ink and blood, lies and intrigue bound tighter than any manuscript.

And among the guests arriving that Monday afternoon; some ambitious, some bitter, some broken, only one had no reason to want Jeremy Pendleton dead.

Pippa Whitcombe was not there for Jeremy. She had a different motive: to find the Mayan Codex she had read of. It would be quite a scoop for the *Gilded Quill*, the university library newspaper. She would return the Codex to its rightful place in the Rare Manuscripts room, but she hoped not before discovering its hidden secrets.

She did not yet know she would be writing the closing chapter of someone's life.

The Gilded Quill

Issue: 234

March 2025

The long-lost Mayan Codex Manuscript, stolen in 1946, may soon be rediscovered, according to recent speculation. Avid investigator and editor of this news sheet, Pippa Whitcombe, has been interviewing former students from the time of its disappearance and is increasingly confident that the manuscript's whereabouts will soon be revealed.

Editor: Pippa Whitcombe

The Vestry Pigeon: Cambridge's Unofficial Mascot

In the heart of Cambridge, perched atop the ancient vestry, lives a pigeon of mystery, resilience, and questionable hygiene. No one knows exactly when it arrived, but it has outlasted generations of students, countless exams, and at least three different coffee shop trends. Some say it's a philosophical bird, contemplating the meaning of existence while staring down at passersby. Others argue it's just waiting for someone to drop a sandwich. Either way, it has become a legend—unmoved by wind, rain, or even the occasional disgruntled professor.

Long may it reign, surveying the city with quiet, feathery judgement.

Bike Thefts increase

Cambridge has long grappled with high rates of bicycle theft, a concern for its many student cyclists. However, attributing this issue to students is misplaced. In fact, students have actively participated in preventive measures. For instance, in November 2024, Cambridgeshire Constabulary marked and registered 590 student bikes to deter thieves.
cambs.police.uk

Moreover, collaborative efforts have led to a 56% reduction in bike thefts since 2018.
cambridge.gov.uk

These initiatives highlight the proactive role of students and the broader community in combating bike thefts, underscoring that students are part of the solution, not the problem.

CHAPTER 1

Ravenshade Manor. Monday 27th October 2025.
Late evening.

Jeremy Pendleton came to with a groan, roused by the heat from an open fire somewhere near— Oh Christ, it was in front of his face. He was lying on the floor and at eye level with the ornamented brass fender surrounding the hearth of the library fireplace. He opened his other eye cautiously and carefully lifted his left hand to push away the lick of hair that blocked his vision; his fingers came away wet from a deep indentation in his forehead. The grate and its blazing coals came into focus and he painfully turned himself over, away from the heat. As he rolled onto his left side, an explosive peal of thunder rolled around the library walls, and he sensed the towering bookshelves shudder around and above, their contents seeming to shift expectantly. The antique plaster busts on top of them grinned mockingly down, their grimaces and the ceiling above them lurching as a wave of nausea overcame him.

He paused for a few seconds and then moved carefully on all fours towards the Chesterfield sofa, remembering to pull up the expensive cloth of his trousers so as to avoid stretching the knees – a laborious but necessary task. Pulling himself up onto the seat, he fought to overcome a desire to vomit.

Steadier now, Jeremy looked around the room. The glow from the wall lamps was soft and highlighted the gleaming porcelain on the mantelpiece. A little Chinese god of longevity appeared to wink at him as a flash of lightning lit up the space which gaped between the heavy, tied-back drapes of the window.

He saw an old, black Bakelite telephone sitting on the desk amongst a confusion of papers, photographs, ink pots, pencils, and a bronze paperweight shaped like a rat. He hoped to God it worked. Making his way unsteadily across the parquet floor, Jeremy sat down heavily on an oxblood-colour winged chair, which sighed gently as it accepted his angular frame.

He heard, with relief, the sound of the rotary dial as it spun and released.

"Which service do you require?"

"Police. Police. I've been assaulted." He waited a few seconds while the call was transferred.

"What is your name and where exactly are you?"

"Jeremy Pendleton. I'm at Ravenshade Manor. I've been hit over the head."

"I'm sorry sir, the line is poor. Where are you? Who is hurt and is a crime in progress?"

Jeremy gritted his teeth and felt a stab of pain and

frustration behind his eyes. He spoke slowly, giving his precise location, and trying to recall what had happened.

He and the anonymous call handler exchanged little more; the storm was causing havoc with communications. But Jeremy was reassured that help would be on the way as soon as possible and he dropped the telephone receiver, which fell over the side of the desk and hung there, suspended by its cord.

He grabbed at the leather desktop in front of him and stood up. Another knife twist of pain skewered his forehead and another clap of thunder barrelled through the room. He needed to get away from Ravenshade. Where were his car keys and belongings – his precious diaries and nascent memoir? He saw again the black, antique telephone sitting squatly on the desk and the straightened cable now trailing over the side, the receiver dangling from it and swinging gently - a dead weight. To his fevered and bludgeoned brain, it looked like nothing so much as a small corpse hanging from a noose.

A surge of fear flooded through him, adding to the swill of disorientation, pain, and sickness in his guts. He thought again that he was going to be sick. He was seven years old and bewildered, crying in the vestry; kneeling before Father Dennis. The priest had just clattered Jeremy across the head for his lack of enthusiasm in responding to his caresses. No! Nobody would see him like this! It was a barely conscious determination. The lonely, bruised, poor little rich kid had spent decades building a carapace so thick and repellent, he would not appear weak now.

It was OK! He had dialled 999. The police were coming. He would be safe from these lunatics. He had fallen against the fender and now he could see where the heavy brass piece had been dislodged. His attacker had lunged at him and together they had tipped forward into the fireplace.

The glow from the wall lamps, mellow as it was, hurt his eyes. Jeremy staggered along the wall to the light switch and turned it off. He was coming round properly now and waited until he could see the desk and chair again in front of the window, which was flexing as wind and torrential rain battered it.

He made his way back to the casement and leaned his forehead gingerly against the glass, before groping his way to the chair and lowering himself gingerly against its high, cool leather back. What was going on here? Figures from his past were dancing a slow waltz in his head. But he had seen them here today, at this writers' retreat he was supposed to be leading (*Oh God, if only I could retreat now!*). Vivienne, Oscar, Alistair and the others. So many of them had reason to hate him.

Another gust rattled the window and Jeremy lifted his head as he heard the door open quietly behind him. In the glass he saw the reflection of a figure slipping into the room. He was not sure if the incomer was human, or divine judgement come at last. He stood up and turned his head as a sheet of lightning lit up the tableau and recognition dawned. "Oh, it's you! Thank God." He looked back towards the window, seeing the reflected figure move closer.

The blow from behind felled him and he sat heavily back into the oxblood chair, which groaned in protest. Blood poured from the back of his head and Jeremy

finally allowed into brief consciousness the deeply buried
certainty that he had spent his life denying. His existence
was an abomination, and he could expect no forgiveness.
The hot coals in the fireplace were as nothing compared
to what he knew awaited him.

Lightning and thunder went unseen and unheard as
they asserted their right to demonstrate the power of the
pathetic fallacy to kickstart a murder mystery.

CHAPTER 2

Parkside Police Station. Monday 27th October 2025. Afternoon.

Detective Inspector Dougie Stevenson leaned back in his chair, eyes drifting from the blinking cursor that punctuated the last sentence of his report. The soft hum of Parkside Police Station buzzed around him, a low murmur of voices and ringing phones. Outside, sheets of rain streaked the windows, the city behind looming grey and unyielding.

Dougie's office was small; just big enough for a desk, a swivel chair, and four sets of filing cabinets. A glass partition wall allowed him a view of his team working hard. He surveyed his desk with its in and out trays, the in tray stacked high and looking ready to topple. Dougie's gaze landed on a small, framed photograph. In it, he had his arm around a petite woman, her hair blowing wild in the wind. They were both laughing. He sighed. It seemed such a long time since he had laughed. He supposed he should get rid of the picture, but he couldn't quite convince himself to do it.

With an effort, he pulled himself back to the present. Three burglaries in as many weeks. Three elderly victims with critical injuries, all now in hospital beds. His gut churned. Whoever was behind these attacks was not just a burglar but a sadist and they were getting bolder. Dougie's phone buzzed. A message from forensics: *Partial match. Suspect identified.* Dougie straightened, his pulse quickening. He typed the final line of the report, his fingers striking the keys with new urgency. The rain outside fell more heavily now, a relentless downpour that mirrored the storm gathering within him. This was not over. Not yet. Until the man – because it was almost certainly a man – responsible was caught, the city's most vulnerable would remain in his sights.

Detective Sergeant Ellie Ford tapped on his door and Dougie beckoned her in with a smile. She was dressed in her usual navy trouser suit, white blouse buttoned up to the neck, and Doc Martens.

"Good news Ellie," he told her. "Forensics have identified our man from partial DNA. We have a name – it's Martin Taylor."

"Richie's brother?" Ellie raised an eyebrow.

"The very same. Their mother must be so proud," answered Dougie wryly.

"Sir," another officer called urgently from his desk, phone pressed to his ear, "it's dispatch, there's a burglary in progress – Arbury Estate, sounds like it could be our man – caller's worried about her elderly neighbour – she lives alone and she can hear screaming and shouting. Uniform are on their way."

"Tell them to head round to the back of the house, we'll head there now." Dougie grabbed his coat from the back of his chair and nodded to Ellie.

DI Stevenson and DS Ford pulled out of Parkside Police Station in an unmarked police vehicle. Ellie had barely pulled her seatbelt across her hips when Dougie swung the car left and headed out towards the location they'd been given.

She had worked in the Met's Specialist Crime Command before transferring to Cambridgeshire. Less adrenaline-fuelled, most of the time, but more scope for promotion. She reached into her trouser pocket for a cigarette and simultaneously remembered she had given up. Instead, she grabbed a lock of hair, twisted it round her finger, and began chewing on it. Dougie, looking straight ahead as he accelerated, grimaced.

"What?" challenged Ellie irritably. "I'm thinking."

There was no answer, nor did she expect one – Dougie listened more than he spoke. They drove on in silence.

Their destination was only two miles away, but it seemed to take forever. Ellie dragged her blonde hair back into a red velvet scrunchie and turned to look behind them. *Where is back up?* she thought anxiously, just as a patrol car came into view. She knew the unmarked paramedic vehicle would not be far behind them.

The terraced house looked much like its neighbours, run-down and with peeling paint on the front door. Ellie saw the patrol car drive past the end of the street. She knew it would turn into the close at the back of the terrace and the uniformed officers would enter through the back of the house.

As Dougie signalled to get out of the car, the front door

to the house opened and a wiry, dark-haired man stumbled out, dropping a phone as he turned to run. Dougie moved quickly. He stuck out his foot as the man ran past then gazed at the man who now lay at his feet, writhing in rage and frustration.

Dougie was mildly impressed at the sheer range of swear words the man pulled from his vocabulary. "Language, Martin…" he tutted.

Suddenly the man was up again, and then somehow there was a knife in his hand, jabbing at Dougie. Ellie did not hesitate. She knocked the knife away and, as the man turned, her knee met his groin with deliberate, satisfying contact. He groaned and crumpled to the ground, defeated. She handed the man over to the uniformed officers now emerging from the front door of the house and they took custody of the still struggling and swearing man.

"You all right sir?" Ellie shouted over her shoulder at her boss as she ran through the front door and straight into a living room where the pale and bloodied face of an elderly woman looked up at her from an armchair.

A few minutes later, they watched the paramedics carry the deeply shocked old lady to an ambulance and only then did they get into their car and drive slowly back to the station. Dougie noticed Ellie's hands tremble slightly as she twisted her hair instinctively towards her mouth again.

"That was quick work back there, Sergeant, well done. Coffee," he said decisively. "We need a coffee – I'll buy. We can plan our interview strategy."

Back at Parkside, Ellie got out of the car and Dougie leaned over the passenger seat, collecting three scrunchies and a hairband from the footwell.

"How many of these blessed things have you got?" he said, throwing them her way.

Back inside, Stevenson called his team together and gave them an account of the arrest. "Right, let's go over the evidence against him again, we want this watertight. I do not want him out again on some technicality. We have a partial DNA match and he's had his fingerprints taken now, so let's see what that throws up. But first, get a good night's sleep all of you, we have a busy day tomorrow. What's up, Ellie? Problem?"

"The suspect will want his duty phone call. He'll want to notify his lawyer. Should we stay and interview him tonight? I don't mind staying late."

"I have considered that, Ellie. We can hold him for twenty-four hours. If we need longer, we can get it, I'm sure." Dougie eyed the worsening weather through the window. "It's been a long week and we all need sleep, so we can think straight."

Ellie raised her hand again. "Nothing to do with the case sir, but I wondered if there was any chance of a lift home? My car gave up the ghost again this morning. The mechanic from the garage said he'll look at it tomorrow." A couple of officers in the briefing room sniggered. Ellie shrugged.

"I'm surprised it's lasted this long," Dougie replied with a smile. "Give me ten minutes and we'll be on our way."

"I'll grab another coffee then while I am waiting. See you in the break room."

From the start, Ellie had looked up to Stevenson. She

admired how he let the work speak for itself. No nonsense. Just determination and clarity. They had built trust slowly; on doorsteps, in interview rooms, while combing through mobile records and CCTV footage. Dougie often let her take the lead, nudging her when necessary. Letting her fall on her face when it would not cause damage. He never made her feel small. He would let her stew then offer a quiet, pointed question. "Did you learn anything from that?" he would ask, tone flat. She would snap back, "Yes." Then softer, "Yeah."

Their relationship was not warm exactly, but grounded in mutual respect. And Ellie needed that. Needed someone who did not care where she came from, or who she loved, or whether she wore lipstick or steel-toe boots. He just wanted her to be good. Sometimes she would catch herself mirroring him: his quiet authority; the way he folded his arms while listening; the directness of his questions.

Dougie leaned against the doorframe of the police station's break room, trying to catch Ellie's eye. He wanted to be away and home before the storm really kicked in. She was laughing with a group of uniforms but looked up and saw her boss waiting for her. Standing abruptly, she made her way towards him, hoping he would play something other than Coldplay in his car.

CHAPTER 3

Ravenshade Manor. Monday 27th October 2025.
Mid-afternoon.

Gina Meredith stared out of the kitchen window at the darkening sky. It was the least grand room at Ravenshade Manor, unseen by guests but homely, with two armchairs by the Aga and an enormous, cluttered pine table where she and Vivienne had spent many long evenings drinking gin.

Gina stretched out her arms above her head and circled her neck – every part of her was tense. They had spent months planning the writers' retreat and there was a lot riding on it. She had been moving furniture all morning, making sure there were enough chairs in the drawing room for this evening's Q and A. She wasn't as young as she used to be, she thought wryly – her hair, piled carelessly on top of her head, was more grey than red these days. Her jeans and sweatshirt were decidedly grubby; she would have to change before everyone arrived.

Gina heard Vivienne hang up the phone and sigh loudly. She raised her eyebrows, "What now?"

"That was Freddie Hughes – she's not coming – the weather is already bad in Scotland, and she doesn't want to risk it. Bloody hell, Gina, she was the main attraction for most people – that book of hers – *Sightless Couriers* – people loved it."

Gina was already moving to the kettle. To her mind, tea solved almost anything – and she didn't want Vivienne to see her worried face.

"Several guests have cancelled too," Vivienne pointed to the typed list of names on the table. At least six were crossed out. The list topped a teetering pile of papers - bills, quotes, estimates for work, lists, recipe books and newspapers. Vivienne dropped into a chair, her purple dress floating down beside her. She scratched the hair under her chiffon headscarf distractedly. "Bloody hell, Gina," she repeated. "This needs to work. We can't give everyone their money back."

Gina narrowed her eyes, pulling two mugs from the Welsh dresser and sitting opposite her friend. "No-one is getting their money back – the Ts and Cs are watertight and, look on the bright side, we won't need to pay Freddie Hughes now."

Vivienne said nothing, wrapping her long fingers round the warm mug. Gina continued, "Jeremy Pendleton can step up, work for his money."

Truth be told, Gina thought Jeremy was well past his prime. His bestsellers had all been from the 90s but with their limited budget a bigger name had been out of reach.

Freddie had been the perfect choice; a young, aspiring author who asked for a very reasonable fee as she was keen for the experience.

Finally, Vivienne replied, "Yes, I'm sure he's up to it and we've got Oscar Double-barrelled-Whatshisname coming from that gallery in Cambridge too – he wants to hold an exhibition here – something about the juxtaposition of old and new art. That would bring in a few extra quid." She made a visible effort to rally and sprung to her feet, "Right, do you think we have enough fizz in the fridge?"

She didn't wait for an answer. "Is it time to heat up the mulled wine? Shall I put on some Fleetwood Mac?"

Gina smiled affectionately at the employer who over the years had become her best friend. Stevie Nicks was Vivienne's idol and her go-to in times of crisis. It was a familiar sound, often drifting out from the camper van where Vivienne chose to sleep, favouring its solitude over the Manor's faded grandeur. Gina knew Vivienne loved Ravenshade fiercely, but still could not quite believe she owned the place, even though it had been 40 years since she inherited it unexpectedly, from a father she had never known.

Gina decided it was best to keep Vivienne busy. "Do you want to do a final check on all the guest rooms – make sure there are flowers, towels, toiletries?"

Vivienne vanished in an instant and although Gina knew she would become distracted along the way, it didn't matter. She had already double-checked everything herself. Details were everything when it came to this retreat being a success and there was such a lot riding on it.

In her nearly twenty years as Estate Manager, Gina had

watched Ravenshade Manor deteriorate year after year and funds were running dangerously low for the essential repairs the house so desperately needed before winter set in. It had taken some work to convince Vivienne of the urgency of the situation. This writers' retreat was the first in a series of planned events aimed at reviving the estate's struggling finances.

Gina shook her head. She couldn't worry about that now, there was still too much to do.

As Gina had predicted, Vivienne was soon distracted from her work and was instead drawn outdoors. A fox stole across the lawn, his dark winter coat disguising him in the shadow of the majestic manor. He heard his vixen's call and set off towards the woods to find her, the dim afternoon light shattered as a conspiracy of ravens rose into the air, a solid blanket of wings. Their deep, rasping calls seemed to suggest an alert to the presence of potential threat.

Vivienne shrilled back to them. "Kraa kraa, be still my protectors..."

She felt a chill in the air. The brewing storm had turned the sky heavy with black clouds, like boulders, threatening to tumble from above any minute. Vivienne hoped the guests would arrive before the deluge.

There was a pungent, earthy scent in the air as she made her way to her campervan to make sure all was secure before heading back to the house.

As she walked, Vivienne ran through the plan in her mind. Gina had asked her to greet the guests as they arrived and direct them to the drawing room, where tea and coffee awaited, until she was ready to show them to their rooms. At 6:30 pm they would be invited to a Welcome reception – mulled wine and canapés – in the drawing room, featuring a Q&A session with the writers… *Writer*, she corrected herself. *Just Jeremy now.* Christ, she hoped he would behave himself.

She was nervous: worried about money; worried that the whole thing might be a mistake; worried about the wisdom of inviting Jeremy here… Ravenshade Manor, of all places.

Back in the lamplit silence of the Entrance Hall, portraits of long-dead ancestors eyed Vivienne's more modern art collection suspiciously. There was a whiff of incense, patchouli, and beeswax in the air. It couldn't quite hide the slight musty smell of the old house. There was the rhythmic, hypnotic ticking of the handsome grandfather clock.

A car pulled onto the gravel drive, tyres crunching loudly over the stones, sharp against the hush of a gathering storm. The first guest had arrived.

CHAPTER 4

Jeremy Pendleton glanced at his watch as he eased the hired Jag across the gravel. It was a pity there was no-one to park the car or help with his luggage, but he had arrived deliberately early; it never hurt to keep people on their toes.

The windows of Ravenshade Manor cast an indifferent gaze on him and Jeremy shrugged in his leather seat. He knew every nook and cranny of this house, where he had spent so many miserable holidays with his uncle and father. He had fully expected to inherit Ravenshade Manor and, at his leisure, hunt for the Codex that his colleagues assumed his father Alfred Pendleton had hidden there. Yet the estate had gone to Vivienne, something he still could not quite believe. There was no doubt it should have remained in the Pendleton family.

Still, so be it! He now had a wonderful opportunity, with the perfect cover of this workshop with its added bonus of explaining to a few of the great unwashed how unlikely they were ever to be published. He never tired of watching the slow dawning of failure and inevitable disappointment on the initially eager and hopeful faces in front of him as he presented them with his own work, reviews, and the Poisoned Chalice awards he had won back in the early 90s. He drew a veil over the following years; in fact he needed to curtain off several decades now, in which his muse had eluded him.

Jeremy unfolded himself from the car, hearing and feeling the twinge of ageing joints. Oh Christ! It was hard keeping this up. How many days was this retreat to be?

Jeremy had thought long and hard before accepting the role of writer in residence; more so than for previous similar offers which he had snapped up when his declining reputation could command a decent fee. His series of crime novels was now in the publishing doldrums of also-rans, being mentioned on the back covers of the latest bestsellers as 'inspiration' or 'early examples of the genre'. He himself needed inspiration to germinate the seed of an idea that had been lodged in his brain for some months. He would finish his autobiography. He would write about his lonely, loveless upbringing, and the redirected retribution he had inflicted upon those around him.

It was quite possible he needed another muse. He had always found it helped if he had someone to use and abuse in order to ignite what creative power he had.

Jeremy bent down awkwardly to check his appearance in the wing mirror. His Adam's apple was prominent against the soft cashmere of his polo neck. His hair was still thick, even if its colour came from a bottle these days. He had not shaved that morning and the stubble, smoothed by balm, had a soft sheen. Straightening up, he told himself,

"You've still got it. Ravenshade can be my muse. Here is where all the secrets, the guilt and the excitement are. They're what holds this building up!"

He would find the Codex, seduce a would-be writer – male, or female – and continue his memoir. He pulled his shoulders back, returned the manor's blank stare, and loped carefully up the steps.

Vivienne had spotted Jeremy as soon as he had got out of the car. She strode across to greet him; intercept him even, before he reached the entrance. He put a wide smile on his face and strode confidently across to her. But then he stopped, discomfited, as she held out a stiff arm, forcing him to take a step back, and shook his hand firmly. He felt that given half a chance she would have turned him round and marched him back down the steps.

Upon seeing Jeremy, Vivienne had felt a wave of intense loathing hit her. Such hatred was not a feeling she was used to, but it infiltrated every part of her.

The forced smile painted across the creased canvas of his face did not fool her. She knew that his charming exterior was the perfect mask to his dark and heartless soul. This man was a manipulator. But she did not want to reveal that she knew his sordid game and so she greeted him in her hospitable way with an equally fake smile. "Welcome, Jeremy. Good to see you, come along in…"

An icy blast followed him inside and as Vivienne pushed the heavy door closed, she noticed the trees outside bending in the wind as if to embrace the ravens who were flying in to hunker down, against the gathering storm.

Gina emerged from the drawing room, hurrying to assist Vivienne with the first arrival.

"Jeremy, this is Gina Meredith, my manager. She will show you to your room," Vivienne said with a warmth in her smile that didn't match the look in her eyes. "Gina, this is Jeremy Pendleton, a friend of old and also our guest speaker for the week."

Whilst Gina was showing Jeremy to his room, Vivienne waited for the next guest. She couldn't help but reflect on the time when, back in the summer of 1979 she had had a brief fling with Jeremy Pendleton. She had been twenty-two. The relationship hadn't lasted very long but she remembered how fiercely she had been attracted to him, how he had looked to her like a classical sculpture. She remembered that twitch at the corners of his mouth. She had found him intoxicating.

She shuddered now, remembering his touch, his sneer, how quickly he had turned from charming to condescending, cruel even. He began to patronise her, demeaning her in front of friends. She ended it then, all trust in him gone.

Vivienne had known Jeremy to be an arrogant prick but continued to put up with him as he was part of her wider social crowd. She had rarely invited him here since she had inherited the place, until today, but Gina had been right. He was a good choice: a well-known name and not too expensive.

Still shuddering, Vivienne tried to compose herself, as she could see their next guest arriving. Taking slow, deep breaths, she reminded herself that of course, Karma would catch up with Jeremy, and it would find him wanting.

Alistair Fradley's journey to Ravenshade Manor had started badly, his stomach lurching as the taxi took the bends at speed. The black faux leather and scent of cheap air freshener had been nauseating. The driver's voice had been a rat-a-tat machine gun of the inane questions that seemed obligatory for the job.

Alistair, though, had been distracted, lost in his thoughts; what the hell had motivated him to agree to the writing retreat? He supposed to support his old friend Vivienne, and to meet the author, Freddie Hughes. But God only knew why he thought himself capable of writing a book. The event was also heavily tainted by the reality of Jeremy Pendleton's attendance. Could he get through a full week in his presence? This was a man he genuinely despised. Jeremy was a dangerous and loathsome individual, who had caused untold devastation and pain not only to Alistair but more importantly to those he loved.

But his thoughts had drifted on to his real motivation for going: the lost Codex. He thought of the card he carried, instinctively patting his jacket pocket. He needed to get into the library at Ravenshade, preferably before Jeremy did. Alistair's pulse quickened in anticipation.

"What about the storm then?" The driver's voice had snapped him out of his reverie. "They reckon it's going to be a biggy, the wife wants me to finish my shift early."

"Yes, that would be wise." Alistair realised he had been

rude. It was not usual for him; he generally struck up conversations wherever he went, much to his partner Peter's dismay. "The Met office has issued a Red Warning, telling people to get off the road."

"Aye that's what she said. Well, guess it will make a change to be early."

And they had eased into an easy conversation about Alistair's old job as an English teacher, his new passion of book dealing, and the forthcoming retreat. The driver vaguely remembered Jeremy Pendleton's books.

"Do you remember that cartoon that was in the paper then? Him in a tutu after that book the Dying Swan had been a flop!"

"He was a laughing-stock! If it happened now, he'd be a meme!" Alistair grinned. Among all of Jeremy's literary works, that book was abysmal; undoubtedly it ranked as the most dreadful book he had ever read. "A murder at the Royal Ballet School… I mean, what was he thinking?"

"Always looked a bit of a posh git to me, I reckon he deserved it," chuckled the driver.

"Yep, couldn't have happened to a nicer bloke," agreed Alistair.

"The wife reads his books. I think they are a load of old tosh personally, not fit to put fish and chips in."

Alistair had nodded in agreement. Inwardly, he felt the glow of satisfaction at the thoughts of Jeremy's failing career. The conversation had culminated in Alistair handing over his card and offering to mail some study information for the driver's son. It was the one part of his old job he missed, supporting the students.

By the time the two old oak trees at the turning to the driveway had signalled their arrival, the wind had already picked up and was whipping across the grounds. The headlights revealed Ravenshade in all her beauty, impressive against the dark autumn sky. A magnificent early Georgian manor house, though slightly weathered, Ravenshade remained true to its original design. The gravel crunched beneath the tyres as the driver navigated his way around the slightly crumbling central fountain. Weathered flagstone steps rose to an imposing stone porch, supported by stone pillars. The heavy oak door held the family crest and intricate black ironwork, including an antiquated bell pull and a raven-shaped knocker. Alistair adored the house: the architecture; the colour of the stone; the feel of the place. The mullion windows flickered a warm welcome.

After bidding farewell to the driver, with his bag deposited at his feet, Alistair had watched the taillights disappear and had lit a cigarette, taking long draws to settle himself.

A shadow flashed in the bay window, and there stood the man himself, Jeremy bloody Pendleton. Alistair's hand instinctively clenched, his jaw tensed, and stomach churned, a response that stayed regardless of time. He knew Jeremy had seen him. What was he thinking?

He vividly remembered the first time he saw Jeremy at Cambridge. Tall, strikingly attractive, perfectly groomed. It wasn't just his looks; the man radiated self-confidence, moved with fluidity. Alistair had been captivated.

As their university lives had continued in similar social circles, Alistair had watched Jeremy, full of entitlement, hurt people he cared about. Over the years, dislike and rivalry had grown into something dark. He had been revelling in Jeremy's fall from favour, the poor book reviews, knowing the man would hate having to tout himself at writing workshops. But it still didn't ease the memories or pain. Unbidden images of his sister Meg's tear-stained face had appeared, along with the old feelings of self-imposed guilt and regret.

Alistair looked up at the sky and let out a long breath. He was not looking forward to engaging with Jeremy again, but he was here now, and stronger, and more importantly he had things to do. He patted his jacket pocket, stamped out his cigarette, retrieved his bag from the ground, and purposefully strode up the steps.

CHAPTER 5

Harrison felt the bedroom at Ravenshade was both their sanctuary and their prison. Neither he nor his wife Madeline were very good at small talk, and they had retreated up here as soon as they could after their arrival.

He looked around at the décor, which should have long since been retired. It was a weary cream and sage green satin paint in an over/under the dado rail design with a splash of William Morris wallpaper, trying hard to cling to the only solid structure it had known, but failing. Harrison couldn't help but feel he was unpeeling too.

His gaze rested on his wife Madeline as she sat at the Georgian rosewood dressing table, the triple mirrors showed different angles of her, and he knew her unease was growing. With each jittery brush stroke her shoulder-length wavy blonde hair bobbed. Her beautiful face was taut as she absentmindedly applied her make-up.

"How are you doing?" he asked as he handed Madeline a glass of her favourite red wine, which they brought from home.

"More nervous than I need to be, as usual," she replied, enjoying an unusually large gulp. "I was so looking forward to a weekend of writing, and now we find out all this…” She waved at the ominous surprise brown package on the bed. That woman – what was her name? Gilly? Gina? – had shown them up to the room and handed them the package, which she said had arrived in the post for them this morning, addressed to Harrison.

“Harrison, it’s just like your sister to buy us this lovely writing retreat gift, then land us with a bombshell of family history to deal with.”

Harrison looked reflective but agreed, “I can’t quite get my head round it. It’s like something out of a novel, all this intrigue, hidden letters, adoption, inheritance…” He eyed the package warily, as if it might explode.

“Harrison, we’re about as comfortable socially as if we were sitting on a wasps’ nest. How on earth are we going to cope?”

“I really need to find out if all this is true, Madeline. I feel like my life, or at least half of it, has been a lie. It’s so soon after Mum’s death and now I find out I was adopted, as well as, all the rest of it…” His voice trailed off and he looked utterly lost suddenly.

Madeline stood, still wrapped in a dressing gown after a quick shower. She needed to close the space between them, reassure him in a physical sense.

“We will. We’ll do this together.” She held his face in her hands, just for a few moments. They moved towards the bed and sat on the fresh white linen cover with embroidered flowers. It was old fashioned but excellent quality, and freshly pressed.

“Maybe the library will have some information about the family tree?” Harrison suggested. “Or we could just ask him outright?”

"Oh God, Harrison. That means confronting him. Can't we just discuss it over dinner?"

"Not sure how well that will work? 'Terrible weather we're having, great main course and by the way I think you may be…'"

"OK, I get the picture," replied Madeline, head in hands.

They both knew they had to keep their anxiety to a minimum or chaos would ensue. They were well aware that wherever they went, they were labelled as 'The Odd Couple'. They were used to it. The truth was, they cherished the small world they had created for themselves. Back home they were in control, with minimal changes and very few surprises.

Together, they discussed everything they had learned from the package. The wine flowed. Madeline asked for help with her dress: a midnight-blue pure raw silk in a simple shift design.

"You look magnificent." Harrison zipped it up, slowly, careful not to catch her skin, kissing the nape of her neck softly, a sign to let her know the task is complete. He placed a necklace around her neck. They both viewed it in the mirror and smiled. It was an antique, a blue and gold butterfly which had belonged to her mother. The blue was the colour of Madeline's eyes.

She slipped a jade bangle on and sprayed herself with Gardenia to complete the outfit. Madeline looked incredible, she just never had the confidence to realise it.

She threaded Harrison's cufflinks through a sharply pressed pure linen white shirt. The links were a pair of books in 18-carat gold, purchased at an antiques fair when they were younger, perfect for the event. Madeline caressed the top of her husband's hand with her thumb: another signal. He studied her face as she concentrated completely on a perfect knot for his navy-blue tie, the ideal match for his sapphire suit. Satisfied, she pulled Harrison towards her for a kiss. His father's old 18-carat Longines watch secured on his right wrist, Harrison was now ready for the night ahead.

As they walked tentatively towards the event, arm-in-arm down the long staircase, uneasy butterflies swarmed inside them both. They pushed the heavy oak doors open to the drawing room, which was already buzzing with anticipation from the other guests. Each step took them closer to an evening they would spend a lifetime having nightmares about.

Just before 6.30, Oscar Martin-Bramston – always punctual - walked down the stairs on his way to the pre-dinner drinks and the question-and-answer session. He was eager to have a good look around, to check out the art and antiques at the manor, hopeful there would be items of interest, but that would have to wait.

He caught sight of himself in the ornate, gilded, pier glass and stopped – *Will Jeremy recognise me?* he thought, *it's been thirty years, more grey hair than black these days, and I've filled out a little.* He felt nervous as he stared at his reflection in the freckled glass. *Come on, get a grip man, you aren't the same person, no longer the shy, unsure youth that Jeremy took great delight in tormenting.*

Oscar took a deep breath, checked his cufflinks, and walked into the drawing room.

He glanced around, automatically assessing the artwork, working the room with a professional eye. The heavy velvet curtains were drawn. An assortment of chairs of various styles was facing the fireplace. He picked up a glass of mulled wine to be polite. He would have preferred a gin and tonic.

The room was almost empty; there was a man gazing at the fire, with his back towards Oscar, a couple chatting quietly, heads bent together and a woman heading towards him from the other side of the room, with a beaming smile.

Vivienne (who looked as bohemian and free spirited as he expected her to be) approached him. "Ah, Oscar. May I call you Oscar? I hope you've settled in. So exciting, the prospect of an art exhibition being held here. I must show you the Old Hunt Room, it's a vast space with brick-vaulted ceilings. It would make the perfect gallery to showcase paintings and indoor sculpture – I know it's difficult to imagine it now, looking out into this raging storm, but our grounds are also an ideal backdrop for outdoor sculpture."

"I'll look forward to seeing it," he replied. "And Oscar is fine."

"Fabulous!" she smiled.

Going to sit down, the man by the fire turned and Oscar recognised a familiar face. "Alistair Fradley!" he exclaimed, smiling. "I haven't seen you for a while, what are you doing here you old rogue?"

"I could ask you the same question. It's good to see you."

Alistair grinned, clapping the other man on the back affectionately.

Oscar and Alistair had met some time ago, both buying and selling small, interesting pieces of art and antiques. Although Oscar was never confident Alistair's business dealings were a hundred percent legitimate, he enjoyed his company. Anyone looking at the two of them together would never have known that they moved in the same circles. Oscar always impeccably dressed, Alistair often crumpled and creased. Oscar always had to fight the urge to trim Alistair's wayward eyebrows.

Mali Pritchard had endured a rain-soaked drive from North Wales to Cambridgeshire and was relieved to see the two stately oaks that flanked the driveway to the Manor. She had deposited her bags in her room and was now in the drawing room, waiting for the Q and A session with Jeremy Pendleton to start.

Vivienne had mentioned to Mali on checking in that Jeremy was now the only speaker as Freddie Hughes, the main speaker on the programme, had cancelled. The forecast severe weather seemed to have resulted in a smaller group for the week. Mali didn't mind too much; she wasn't planning to write a bestseller and didn't know the work of Freddie Hughes, but she did want to speak with Jeremy Pendleton, preferably just the two of them. She was, however, disappointed that having only one speaker might limit her opportunities for speaking with him. She would have to think carefully when to make her approach.

Mali gratefully accepted a mulled wine offered by Vivienne. She could see canapes on the side but felt it rude to be the first to help herself. Two men were in the room; one was Oscar, who was dapper in his dress and appeared very pleasant. The second was Alistair, who had just stepped up to say hello. There was also an attractive middle-aged couple, seated by the fire, murmuring quietly to one another. *Expensive dress*, pondered Mali, admiringly. This writing retreat really had attracted all sorts. She had noticed the couple earlier that afternoon when they arrived, just after her. She guessed these were Mr and Mrs Chester, the only couple on the guest list.

After she had checked in, she had left her bags in the hall and was helping herself to a coffee in the drawing room, when she noticed the couple arrive. The door to the hallway stood open and she had been admiring an unusual umbrella stand, made from metal and shaped like a black bear. The man had been carrying the bags and had his other arm around his wife. *That's rather nice*, mused Mali. They had seemed to be taking the stairs carefully, as if walking on red-hot coals. This was understandable, thought Mali. Visiting somewhere different and old like Ravenshade made you feel as if you were walking into living history.

Mali turned her attention back to the present. A fierce gust of wind and rain rattled against the windows and the heavy curtains ballooned into the warm space, bringing a momentary chill with them. She noticed Oscar shiver. The door opened again, and Jeremy Pendleton walked in.

He didn't make eye contact with anyone but strode confidently forward and sat in a large green leather button-back armchair at the front of the room, his back to those present. He was an imposing figure, she supposed. About seventy, but still upright, tall and aloof.

Mali had only read one of Jeremy's books and she certainly felt life was too short to worry about reading any more, but everyone seemed oddly hypnotised by this new arrival. Jeremy himself was leaning forward in his chair in anticipation of his drink, posed as if for a portrait. He turned his head slowly and with an appraising eye, looked everyone up and down. His eyes lingered on Harrison Chester and his expression was sneering. *What an unpleasant man*, Mali thought. He could be a little more appreciative that anyone was here at all, given the weather. She found herself turning to look again at the couple. They definitely seemed tense and sat very close to each other. Mali didn't feel exactly relaxed herself. She had brought a supply of various home-grown and dried herbs with her, ready for any situation that might arrive. As she looked round the room, she decided they could all do with a good cup of chamomile tea. Nobody looked very comfortable.

By 6:30 pm, all but one of the guests were gathered in the drawing room. Apart from Harrison and Madeleine, who sat whispering quietly together in their seats, they were all standing in the glow of the blazing open fire, the logs crackling and spitting. The heat seeped into them, mingling with the pleasant effects of the mulled wine, and they began to relax.

Ancestral portraits gazed disdainfully down on them from one wall, sitting in judgement of these inferior commoners. On other walls Vivienne had been gradually replacing forlorn landscapes with colourful artworks painted by local creatives whose work she wished to promote. Their bright abstracts were clearly at odds with the rest of the ancient décor, but she felt that an eclectic mix improved the ambience of the staid old place.

Slowly, almost reluctantly, those gathered left the warmth of the fire behind and began taking their seats for the presentation that was due to start.

CHAPTER 6

Pippa Whitcombe had stepped into the manor, late as usual. A breath of cool air greeted her, carrying the faint scent of polished wood and old stone. Wearing her signature embroidered tailcoat with deep pockets and baggy, worn-at-the-knees jeans, she carried her usual air of effortless disarray. Her dark skin and wide green eyes made a striking contrast, often prompting the familiar question, "Where are you from?" to which she always replied, with a wry smile, "Cambridge."

The vast hallway stretched out before her, its grandeur softened by a faded Persian rug that lay worn yet dignified beneath her feet. She could not help but be impressed. A fusty old house was the best place to find lost treasures; her investigatory instinct was heightened.

A huge gilt-framed mirror loomed on the far wall. Georgian pier glass, Pippa suspected. *Pricey.* Its surface dimly reflected the light glistening through the tall windows. In the centre of the space stood a heavy circular wooden table, the wood polished so the wear showed years of love. It was proudly adorned with an urn overflowing with autumnal flowers. Their rich, fiery hues stood in striking contrast to the room's muted elegance. There was definitely someone with taste living here. However faded the grandeur, the softened state spoke of someone who loved beauty, and cared for the place, equally deeply.

The air held the weight of memory and hushed stories. Pippa felt it, a soul, lingering just below the surface. Having paused to decide where to go and what to do with her carpet bag, she heard voices drifting in from just beyond the entrance hall. Pippa began to wonder who had already arrived and checked in. Her nerves flickered, just for a moment, and she drew in a deep breath before walking towards the chatter, carpet bag and contents in toe.

Get this over with, Pippa Whitcombe, she told herself and gave herself a little shake. *You are here for one reason and one reason only.*

She followed the sound of the voices, through oak doors at the far side of the hall. She pushed the door open to see they were already seated in a loose semi-circle presumably for the impending author talk. As she stepped inside the room, every face turned toward her; some smiling, others unreadable.

This was going to be a fascinating week, she could feel it. Her head buzzed with anticipation. She already had a few solid clues jotted down in her trusty notepad, and she was determined to piece them together. The people gathered here were part of the trail leading to the missing Mayan Codex. They were also all older than her by at least ten years.

A tall, attractive man in his late sixties eyed her lazily. There was something familiar about him… Jeremy

Pendleton, she guessed. He looked just like Alfred Pendleton, the esteemed professor at the university at the time the Codex went missing. He would have been this man's father. Erm, interesting. Her pen was itching to write down these impressions but, clutching her bag at her side, she felt the host was homing in on her.

Vivienne knew immediately who this young woman must be; she was the last guest to arrive. "Come in, come in. Welcome to Ravenshade, Pippa," she said warmly, her voice carrying easily over the gentle murmur of conversation. "Let me get you a mulled wine."

Pippa smiled and walked towards the others, finding a free chair and plonking herself down, the carpet bag at her feet.

Vivienne began the introductions. Firstly Gina Meredith, who was the estate manager and who told Pippa that she would show her to her room later. Gina seemed at ease in her position and Pippa felt the two of them were firm friends, the energy between them was very much 'We've got this'.

The polo-neck-clad older man still had his eyes on Pippa. Vivienne waved a hand in his direction, saying, "That's Jeremy, he's the speaker," with such casual dismissal Pippa could tell she wasn't a fan. The resemblance was remarkable; Jeremy had the distinct look of his father. His eyes followed Pippa as Vivienne introduced her to the other guests.

Alistair Fradley had the appearance of an ageing hippy, with his bohemian style of dress, an unshaven face, and a chiselled jawline. His clothes hung loosely from his frame, giving him a slightly shapeless silhouette. Yet there was something in his eyes – a sharpness – that suggested intelligence. The way he held his glass, fingers tight around the stem, he sat forward in his chair, like he was eager to comment at some point. It was clear to Pippa that he was on edge. He acknowledged her with a small nod of his head.

To the right of Alistair sat a couple, their chairs pushed together. Harrison and Madeline Chester. Madeline leaned into Harrison with every breath, their dynamic striking Pippa as a seesaw of complexity, subtle yet telling. They were dressed smartly and with care, their outfits complementing each other in coordinated tones. Interestingly Madeline, who sat with her legs crossed, wore extremely high heels; a choice that seemed at odds with her otherwise modest and composed demeanour. The couple inclined their heads at the same time, and smiled a greeting.

Pippa instinctively suspected they had little genuine interest in writing and could not help but wonder if their presence hinted at some connection to the Codex. Time, she knew, would reveal more.

On the other side of Alistair sat an intriguing figure, holding his glass delicately by the stem in total contrast to Alistair. Pippa found herself naturally drawn to him. He was impeccably dressed, with a thick swatch of grey hair swept neatly back. His face was calm, marked with thoughtful lines that suggested a lifetime of experience. He struck her as a quiet fountain of knowledge. Though he appeared reserved, there was a flicker of mischief in the slight smile he offered as Vivienne introduced them. His name was Oscar Martin-Bramston, an art dealer by profession, and already Pippa was intrigued. She silently hoped she might be seated next to him at dinner.

Mali Pritchard, who looked every bit the delicate flower, was very attractive with an urchin haircut, cut sharp to her face and accentuating her cheekbones. She was dressed in soft cashmere and tailored tweed trousers, petite with a grounded, earthy presence. There was a warmth to her that immediately set Pippa at ease.

Mali stood up and greeted the younger woman with genuine delight, her soft Welsh tones soothing after the slightly charged energy of the room. *A normal person*, Pippa thought, *thank goodness*. Mali would be something like a thespian, she guessed; there was something expressive and quietly luminous about her.

It was, without a doubt, an interesting mix of people. And already, Pippa had identified at least three who might share her goal, or at the very least, have a lead on the long-lost Mayan Codex and where it might have been hidden all these years in Ravenshade Manor. Pippa's natural instincts to get to the truth and her perception in reading the room gave her that tingle of excitement again. She had a strong feeling this was going to be one holy fuck of a few days.

Vivienne clapped her hands to gain attention, asked if everyone had a drink, and pointed out the canapes on the side. With a radiant smile on her face, she announced: "Gina and I are thrilled and excited to welcome you all to join us for this creative journey here at Ravenshade Manor – our comfortable home. We are especially pleased that you managed to battle the elements to arrive today. We trust you found your rooms to your satisfaction. If there is anything you require, simply ask. Gina and I are available to help throughout your stay and can answer any questions or concerns. Unfortunately, a few participants

- along with Freddie Hughes, our main tutor for the week - have had to cancel due to the treacherous road conditions. However, the upside of this is it means it will be a very intimate experience with more individual attention for you all. I believe it was predestined by the universe all along. I encourage you all to approach the retreat with an open mind and heart, ready to embrace new experiences and teachings. Over the coming days we will engage in a variety of creative writing exercises, workshops and readings, with time and space to write and reflect. I hope you find inspiration to unleash your inner writer. There is also free time scheduled in to immerse yourselves in the beauty and tranquillity of our historical Estate, to visit Cambridge, or to simply relax in these idyllic surroundings. The Agenda sheets give a detailed timetable of events, and can be found on the chiffonier over by the window on the left. They give a timetable of talks and mealtimes – ahh yes, our healthy and nourishing menus will definitely delight your tastebuds! It is now my pleasure to introduce my long-standing friend, esteemed author, writer of several bestsellers, twice winner of the 'Poisoned Chalice Award' for Crime Writing, our guest author Mr Jeremy Pendleton who has kindly agreed to take up the mantle of Main Tutor for the retreat workshops."

Whilst Vivienne introduced Jeremy, he waved his fingers idly in a consciously self-deprecating acknowledgement as she listed his books and awards.

Mali was sure she heard Alistair groan and there was no ripple of polite applause; just a palpable sense of disappointment and tension. The room clearly wasn't full of the Jeremy Pendleton fan club.

She heard Oscar sigh quietly and murmur to Alistair, "Oh joy, no Freddie, and we are about to receive words of wisdom from the largest ego in the room."

CHAPTER 7

"Perhaps I should stand." Jeremy rose, looking at the faces around him.

Well, Oscar thought, *his voice is the same, that rich baritone hasn't changed. He must dye his hair, though.* He noted too that Jeremy's face was etched with lines of unkindness that told the story of his life; there was no sign of laughter lines, or warmth, there.

All eyes were focused on Jeremy, but some looked tense; hostile, even.

"Thank you, Viv, and Ms Meredith, for having approached me to lead this workshop. I understand I was not your first choice, but I shall put that down to your financial priorities rather than any lack of discernment. My first piece of advice is to read, and read greedily. Wolf down all you can, across genres and ages. You may find it saves you a lot of trouble. Most things worth saying have been said before, and said better than you can ever hope to express. The old adage to would-be writers is to begin with what you know. I agree. Looking around, I suggest you begin simply. I suppose you must all have some experiences you are keen to share with the rest of the world, no matter how insignificant they might appear."

Jeremy moved on to talking about himself and his esteemed literary career.

Mali's stomach growled loudly, reminding her she hadn't eaten for some time. She looked up from her notebook, sensing eyes on her. Jeremy was staring at her as if she were like something unpleasant on the bottom of his shoe.

"Sorry," she said, surprised at hearing her own voice. "That was my stomach, obviously, I mean of course it was my stomach, not … I haven't eaten for a while. Sorry Jeremy… everyone."

Jeremy's Adam's apple looked tense, its shape protruding through his polo neck, and his pursed lips ready to spit venom. She noticed just a brief smile on Oscar's face and Alistair seemed amused. "Sorry Jeremy," Mali repeated, feeling unusually embarrassed and belittled by this man, even though he had not uttered a word to her. She thought of her brother, Owain, in the presence of this man. He was formidable to her as an adult. What on earth would he have seemed like to a young boy? Mali wanted to believe that Owain's fatal accident had nothing to do with the man in front of her but the more time she spent in his presence, the more she began to believe he was capable of anything to further his own literary career.

Mali picked up her notebook from her lap as the droning voice of Jeremy started up once again, repeating like a worn-out mantra how a successful author like himself draws on all of life's experiences, good and bad, to inform their stories. *I bet you do*, thought Mali. *Surely we will have time soon to ask our questions.*

"If you want to be a successful writer, you need to harden your heart and never let personal sensitivities get in the way of a good story or character. Keep a diary and plunder it for ideas." He flourished a cheap exercise book he'd taken from his pocket. "Mine comes everywhere with me; I've got scores of them now. Some of you may end up in this one, who knows? Use people and experiences for plot fodder. I am writing my memoirs currently and these books have proved very useful." He noted the look of surprise on the faces before him – all focused on the tatty, dog-eared item in his raised hand. "It's what's in there that counts! All the calfskin and woven paper in the world won't make a great author." He saw, with some pleasure, the frisson of distaste that greeted his mention of baby cows in such a context.

Jeremy turned to Gina, who was heading towards him with a tray. "I asked for a single malt." She nodded and handed him a double in a sparkling crystal glass, then retreated out of the room, glad to be out of there.

Jeremy took a sip, smacking his lips. It was not the best whisky he had tasted, but it would do. "And now to questions."

The question that sprung to Oscar's mind was – *Why are you such an arrogant bastard?* But he didn't think it would be appreciated. *Best keep that one for later.*

A number of hands went up. Jeremy homed in on Pippa. "You. Who are you and why are you here?"

"My name is Pippa Whitcombe, I'm not here to get writing tips. I'm a reporter with the Cambridge student newspaper *The Gilded Quill*. I was hoping to interview you about the Mayan Codex that your father Alfred was entrusted with when it vanished in 1946. Some believed your father knew the truth. Did he confide in you? Do you know what happened? Do you know where it might be now?"

Jeremy's face darkened. He spoke slowly and forcefully, "I do not offer 'writing tips' as you call them. And as to the Codex, I do know of it and that is the full extent of my knowledge. I am not my father. Let's not bore our fellow guests with irrelevant speculation. I shall not be giving you an interview and I suggest if that is the sole reason for your presence here, you might as well leave now and let those with literary ambition have the floor."

Oscar looked at Pippa. She didn't seem fazed and she continued to look at Jeremy. *She may be young but she's clearly tough. I'd have been so upset at her age*, he thought, admiring her resilience and bravery.

Mali had to control herself. How could this old, decrepit has-been speak to the young woman like that? Pippa had arrived to the Q&A only slightly late. The weather was worsening and she must have had a bad journey, poor thing. Mali recognised the alpha male needed to dominate someone in the room; he was a bully and chose easy prey, but he had miscalculated this time. She stared at Pippa, with some admiration – the younger woman stared at Jeremy, completely unruffled, Mali turned her attention back to Jeremy, the withered old prick, telling herself to keep focused and not get distracted. She realised Jeremy was speaking to her.

"I'm Mali Pritchard. We have never met, but my grandparents were at Cambridge at the same time as your father in the late 1940s, they were friends and you would have met my parents when they were younger. My question is about developing a plot. My brother attended one of your sessions at a school creative writing weekend, back in 2012. You may remember it… mid Wales, Builth Wells? He, Owain, was writing a book based on our father's tales of grand old houses and hidden treasure, he called it 'Truth and Treasure in the Stones.' My brother liked to believe there was an element of truth in his stories. Owain was forever scribbling down tales and ideas in his own notebooks – much like you have advised aspiring writers to do this evening." She smiled at him tightly before continuing. "He was excited to be sharing his drafts with you, as an established author. What is your view on using material heard from those attending such courses for the author's own ends, whether from adults or children? Theft, do you think? Unethical certainly? Is it something you have found yourself doing, inadvertently of course; perhaps even unconsciously?"

Jeremy cleared his throat and when he began to speak, he appeared to be addressing her chest, rather than her directly. When he lifted his eyes from her chest his stare was so intense she thought she might burst into flames. He recovered quickly.

"That would be totally inappropriate and lead into all sorts of legal battles. However, one gathers all sort of details, snippets and tales throughout one's life which should be garnered in and used to inform or shape our writing. Many tales would never see the light of day as so many do not have the skills to use such material or, in the case of your brother, perhaps, never had the opportunity. Have you read my earlier books? Of course you have."

"I may have read one or two. My brother, sadly, did not

return home following a fatal accident on the creative writing course. You may remember that terrible event?'

"Sadly not. Life is busy. Next question." He turned back to the others in the room.

Mali felt sure he did remember and that he may well know something about her brother's death. The police had not interviewed Pendleton at the time, despite the fact that he had been the last person to see Owain alive. Her family wanted answers: how had Owain been before the accident; what had happened to his notebooks… anything to make sense of his death. Mali was ten years older than her brother and wanted her parents to have some closure, even if nothing would bring Owain back. The week had only just begun though, there was still time.

Alistair was becoming increasingly agitated with every word that came from Jeremy's mouth. Without waiting to be invited to ask a question, he spoke through gritted teeth, "Some of your characters are particularly nasty, hateful, damaged individuals. Where do you get your inspiration?"

Jeremy appeared to recognise him, there was a small tic at the side of his jaw, but then he smirked,

"Well, Alistair, is it? I look for possibilities in my characters rather than moral reckonings. I find inspiration in people and the encounters one has in life. Some are intriguing, sexy, dangerous, and exciting. Others are infinitely… infinitely forgettable."

Those last few words were drawn out as he held Alistair's gaze.

Oscar found himself holding his breath. The atmosphere in the room was tense and electric, mirroring the storm outside. He was sure Alistair was going to launch himself at Jeremy, he had never seen anyone so angry. Vivienne put her hand on Alistair's arm to try and calm him.

Meanwhile, the Chesters were becoming increasingly frustrated. In their slightly nervous, awkward way, they had been trying to get Jeremy's attention since the start of the session, popping up and down like meerkats. Finally they both stood and practically shouted his name.

He looked at them, raised an eyebrow, sipped his whisky. "Yes?"

The woman sat down, whispering, "Sorry."

The man remained standing, however, and spoke hesitantly, "Er, Harrison, We hear very little about your family; your influences, who have been the loves of your life? Do you have any children?"

Jeremy remained silent, and took another sip of his whisky. Harrison tried to clarify, "What I mean is, your past influences your present, the person, I mean, writer you become, doesn't it? It shapes you."

Unexpectedly, Jeremy laughed loudly, shook his head, and to no one said in particular said, "Where do we find them? Well, Mr Harrison—"

Harrison's' wife nervously interrupted, "It's just Harrison. Harrison Chester."

Jeremy dismissed her with a wave of his hand. "If I do decide to divulge details about my personal life, you shall be the first to know." He took another swig of whisky, emptying the glass.

There was a silence, which stretched on for several moments, all eyes seeming to avoid those of Jeremy, who stood with a sneer on his face and an upward tilt to his chin, seeming to dare anyone else to ask a question.

With perfect timing, the door opened and Gina announced brightly, "Ladies and gentlemen, dinner is ready, if you'd like to make your way to the dining room."

Oscar breathed a sigh of relief. Thank God that session was over, Jeremy was more arrogant than ever, so cruel. It seemed as if almost everyone there had some sort of unpleasant past connection to Jeremy, and what on earth had got into Alistair? What was that about?

When Pippa mentioned the Codex, Oscar had been sure that was why Alistair was there, it was just the sort of thing he would be interested in. That level of anger, though. He was seething, there must be something else to it. *These next few days are going to be hell,* thought Oscar. *Jeremy has no fans here and it seems as though he's made a number of enemies over the years. I need a drink.*

CHAPTER 8

In the kitchen, Gina took a deep breath. "Calm down woman, it's only dinner for eight," she thought out loud, muttering to herself, "Piece of cake… well, not actually cake, it's meringue."

Her tongue stuck out as she concentrated on putting the last of the raspberries on top of the elaborate three-tier pavlova she had constructed to be the dinner's finale. She was giving the guests in the dining room a few minutes to find their seats, pour the wine, settle in; there had been a terrible atmosphere in the drawing room when she went in to announce dinner was ready.

She had chosen a deliberately simple menu – soup with broccoli from the garden, sweet potato tagine (because it was Vivienne's favourite), and the pavlova with the autumn raspberries from the bushes by the kitchen door – the ones the birds hadn't eaten.

She had already rejigged all the place settings – she had thought the table looked a bit spartan with so many missing guests, so she had picked the last of the roses before the wind got up and arranged them in china bowls down the length of the Georgian dining table, after covering its walnut surface with a pretty linen tablecloth she had found in the attic – a rare one with no mouse damage. The heavy velvet drapes were drawn against the storm that was building outside and there were lit candles in two large candelabras, decorated with ravens and berries. Yes, she thought, it would do. The soft light hid the couple of places where the wall was water-damaged – evidence of the leaking roof.

She had put Vivienne at one end and Jeremy at the other – best to keep those two well apart. She thought Vivienne would like the reassurance of Alistair close by, so seated him on her right and Mali to her left. She had put Pippa to Alistair's right – she liked that girl, she had a twinkle in her eye and was clearly a smart young woman. Alistair would enjoy her company. She had placed Oscar next to Jeremy – he looked like a worldly person who would not be easily intimidated by Jeremy's nonsense. The Chesters were opposite Oscar and Pippa; she thought they seemed nervous and perhaps a bit lacking in social skills, so best to seat them together.

Gina had made space on the kitchen table, by sweeping all of the teetering piles of papers, books and other junk onto the dresser. She moved her favourite pink vase with more care. She had plonked a few roses in it earlier, left over from her dining room flower arrangements. The table was now clear to plate up the meal. She topped the last of the soup bowls with a swirl of cream and a few crumbs of blue cheese, picked up the tray, and headed for the dining room.

The atmosphere in the dining room was subdued when she entered, it was that point in the evening when everyone was sizing each other up.

Vivienne was talking a little too loudly to Alistair, "Ali, be a darling and be in charge of wine tonight, there's plenty on the sideboard and we can bring up some more if we need it – I inherited the cellar with the house, we might as well enjoy it!"

Gina saw Jeremy roll his eyes and heard him murmur, "How vulgar."

"I beg your pardon?" Vivienne called down the table, sensing his tone, rather than the actual words, Gina thought. "Gina, do serve our Guest Speaker first."

Gina could not help but admire her boss, every inch the hostess, her hair piled up messily now, tendrils falling out of the inevitable chiffon scarf, looking much younger than her sixty-eight years, in another delicate dress, this time peacock-blue.

"No, no, ladies first," Gina replied, serving Vivienne and making her way around the table to each female guest.

Madeline picked up the bread roll from her side plate, "Is this gluten free?" She sniffed it suspiciously.

Gina smiled professionally, whilst Jeremy proffered an incredulous sneer. "Oh God, vulgar and vexatious," he muttered.

"I don't recall seeing that you required a gluten-free option on your dietary requirement form, Mrs. Chester." Although she did recall that the woman was allergic to pineapple, mushrooms, and shellfish.

Madeline sniffed, "Well, I'm not gluten intolerant, I just prefer not to overload my digestion."

Jeremy nearly choked on the whisky he had brought to the table and hastily coughed.

"Well, these were homemade this morning, full of seeds

and olives, very good for the digestion, I'm sure," Gina
replied briskly, before moving on to serve the rest of the
table.

Whilst she cleared the soup bowls twenty minutes later,
Alistair was topping up glasses enthusiastically.

"Lovely little Sancerre, this." His cheeks were turning
pink, and Gina was sure he had already thoroughly tested
all the whites on offer. She eyed the sideboard; she would
pop down to the cellar before dessert.

"Beautiful soup," said Mali politely, leaning backwards
slightly to let Gina pick up her bowl. "What is that blue
cheese… gorgonzola?"

"No, Perl Las – it's Welsh, believe it or not!"

Mali clapped her hands together gleefully.
"Carmarthenshire!" she exclaimed. "That place is
amazing – their organic farming means the place is alive
with wild herbs, grasses – the diversity!"

Vivienne and Mali began talking animatedly about
herbs. Gina picked up the last of the bowls. *She's a
handsome woman*, she thought admiringly about Mali. *Good
clothes, understated, classic.*

Oscar caught Gina's eye. "Cambridge Cheese
Company? That Perl Las? I buy all my cheese there."

"You have good taste." Gina took in his smart jacket
and perfectly pressed shirt. Good manners, good taste,
and a sharp dresser. She approved.

Gina brought in the main course in two large
earthenware pots, placing them in the centre of the table,
to allow guests to serve themselves. The meal was
deliberately informal, giving everyone a chance to chat
and get to know each other as they helped one another to
food. Family service, they had called it at primary school.

Gina removed the lid of the tagine closest to Jeremy, aromas of harissa and coriander rising on the steam. The writer helped himself enthusiastically, whilst to his right, Madeline tried to engage him in conversation,

"My husband's father," she faltered, flicking a glance at her husband, "Well, his adoptive father was Grayson Chester, he wrote 'My Sojourn in the Sahara'….."

Gina caught a glare from Jeremy of such ferocity that Madeline seemed to shrink in her seat. Gina's stomach grumbled, reminding her that she had not eaten since breakfast time. She moved around the table, checking with a practised eye that everyone had what they needed, and was amused to hear Vivienne and Mali still engrossed in conversation.

"I'm experimenting with 'electuary', a mix of honey and dried herbs – a honey pill – what I really need is a beehive!" Mali exclaimed excitedly.

"You need to come and see my Still Room and Walled Garden once this storm passes," Vivienne said.

"Dear God!" Despite his enthusiasm just moments earlier, Jeremy took a theatrical sniff at his full plate. "Am I about to partake of a bowl of compost? Really?" he asked of Vivienne as he glared at her down the table.

You know exactly what you are doing, thought Gina. *Playing the room, making sure you are the centre of attention.*

"Oh, Jeremy, you know I'm a vegetarian, we never have meat here," Vivienne admonished mildly, but her face was stony.

Oscar leaned towards Jeremy, clearly eager to diffuse the tension. "Are you hoping to solve the Codex mystery whilst you're here?"

Jeremy turned to his neighbour, grimacing with irritation at another question about the wretched Codex, but the stock dismissal died on his lips as he saw an attractive and confident man looking at him with genuine curiosity. His down-turned mouth lifted into a smile, "That all happened in my father's time and I don't bathe in his questionable glory. Might I ask, do you have a research interest in such artefacts? You have the look of a cultured man." As Jeremy studied the face before him, Gina saw recognition dawn. "Oscar! is it really you?"

"Yes, it's really me, older and much wiser, and I'd like to take this opportunity to thank you for the role you played in my growing up."

Gina heard and watched this exchange with interest as she hovered near the doorway. She saw Jeremy's normally self-satisfied expression dissolve into something more uncertain. "Oh?" he queried cautiously. "I recall we had rather a ball for a term or two."

"I suppose we did," Oscar replied steadily. "Until your unique talent for humiliation allowed you to drop me like an old toy. You even tried to have me sent down."

Gina could see that Jeremy was rattled. She also saw confirmation that here was a monster of manipulation and disregard of others' feelings. She was thrilled to hear Oscar follow through in a quietly confident, almost rehearsed, tone, "Because of your callous behaviour, I learned to recognise the opposite – integrity and loyalty. I've had a wonderful relationship with someone who understood what true love is and because of that support I have a fulfilling career and some status in the art world. You have a perverted idea of love and look at you now. You are a has-been of a writer and an ageing Lothario. I can see you haven't changed and quite honestly your behaviour looks ridiculous now. You're as dated and tattered and incomprehensible as that Codex must be, if it still exists. Sadly, you do."

Gina saw Jeremy reel back as if he had been physically assaulted, but he quickly reasserted himself. "Well, well, Oscar. I must have taken a big bite of you when we were young. Haven't forgotten, have you? Good to hear you're still dabbling in art."

While this was going on, Alistair had drifted, conversations flitting around him with a constant hum. He was mulling over meeting Pippa later and her intention to find the Codex. Initially he'd had reservations about joining forces with her, but her enthusiasm and energy were growing on him. Having chatted to her for a while now, he understood three things:

With or without him, she was going to look for and discover the Codex; after years of searching he instinctively sensed that its time had come. She had a keen investigative mind and had already deduced details he had missed. Like him, she was intent on returning the Codex to its rightful place, the university library.

Finally he knew they needed some help, a look-out. Someone who could be trusted and possessed knowledge of history and art. Oscar was that person and would want to stop Jeremy getting his hands on it.

" So you think it's definitely here then?" Pippa asked in a hushed voice.

"Yes, I heard his darkness over there talking about it when he was drunk at a party." Alistair tipped his head in

Jeremy's direction. "We need to get to it before he finds it and sells it to the highest private bidder."

Pippa nodded, a hint of a smile on her face. "Agreed, do you think it's in the Ravenshade library? That is my thinking, that is where we need to start."

"Yes. I think you are right, we need to keep Pendleton away from it." He started to move his chair back. "Better get back on wine duty. But have a look at this." He slid a crumpled piece of paper across the starched tablecloth. "It's the riddle that was in the pack of information I found. See what you think. I also have this tarot card, which I think is an important link but can't quite work out how yet."

Gina watched Alistair as he sauntered around the table with the wine bottle before leaning in to talk to Oscar.

When he returned, Alistair said to Pippa, "Oscar says he'll join us. I know we can trust him and could certainly do with his experience," he whispered as he poured wine into her glass.

"We need to agree a time and place to meet," said Pippa. "I think early hours when everyone is in bed. Give me your phone number, I will get Oscar's too, and set up a group chat for us to message discreetly."

The noise in the room grew as Gina served the pavlova. Alistair was pouring dessert wine with gusto, pressing it on an unwilling Mali, who was covering her glass with her hand. "I just don't like it; it reminds me of cough medicine."

Jeremy had got up from his seat; not enough adoration at that end of the table for his liking, Gina suspected. Oscar was deep in conversation with Pippa, and the Chesters had their heads together, talking quietly.

Jeremy threw himself into Alistair's seat and rudely interrupted Oscar and Pippa's conversation. He was soon rattling on to Pippa about Cambridge student life in his day. "God, the May Balls, the survivors' photographs, always up 'til dawn. Always plenty on offer if you know what I mean. I remember one year, I met these two girls, identical twins they were…"

Gina could tell from Vivienne's face that she was distressed by his sleazy turn in the conversation. She put a hand on Vivienne's shoulder and squeezed. "OK?"

Vivienne pulled Gina towards her until her mouth was close to Gina's ear, "Can you believe I fell for his crap? I know I was young, but still, it makes me shudder just thinking about it now."

Gina said nothing, just squeezed her friend's shoulder a little more tightly.

Alistair had made his way back to his seat next to Vivienne, now filled by Jeremy. He was a little unsteady on his feet now but his voice was ringing as he clapped Jeremy heavily on the back, "You are in my seat and," he paused, his voice loud and getting harsher, so the whole room fell silent, "you are being offensive."

Gina cut across the silence that followed. "Ladies and gentlemen, coffee and drinks will be served in the drawing room, if you'd like to head that way."

CHAPTER 9

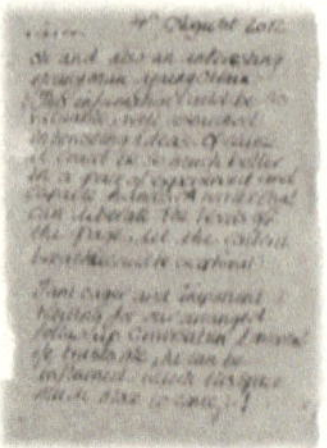

As they left the dining room, Vivienne grabbed Alistair's hand, "Come on Ali darling, let's go for a smoke." They grabbed coats and Alistair picked up a brolly from the antique bear stand in the hallway. As they opened the door, the brolly was instantly blasted inside-out.

"Let's go into the old hunt room, it's dry in there," shouted Vivienne.

They darted across the driveway into the outbuilding for their cigarette and a good old sound off about their despicable acquaintance Jeremy.

Jeremy excused himself straight after dinner and headed to the library, supposedly to prepare for the following morning's workshop. "Please do not disturb me, I need time alone to think," he said, wafting his hand in the air dramatically. Gina handed him another large whisky as he passed and he took it, then took the bottle as well, looking straight ahead with no word of thanks. He was not one for small talk with the untalented and he had no intention of getting embroiled in offering one-to-one guidance, although Pippa was youthful and looked like a bit of guidance might not be a bad thing. The Welsh girl also looked like she had been waiting all her life for a well-educated, experienced Englishman. Mind you, now he knew her family connections, he might be wiser to stay out of her way. *Still, plenty to keep me busy over the weekend,* he mused as he left the room.

Jeremy closed the door to the library and surveyed the room. It was just how he remembered it. He ran his hands over the old bookshelves and took in the smell of parchment, echoes of memories. What was going on? How could Vivienne, Oscar and Alistair all be here at the same time? Circling like a carousel of ghosts from his past. He had said his penance many times, he knew that, but he crossed himself for reassurance.

With some effort, he turned his mind to the Codex. It was one of the reasons he had been persuaded to come here. He wanted that manuscript and it was clear that Pippa was also determined to find it. The library was exactly the sort of place where his father might have hidden it - amongst all those books and documents, hiding in plain sight! The old bastard! Was there a safe in here, or a secret door? He couldn't remember. Peace, time to think and look around, were exactly what he needed. He poured himself another drink, grimacing as he swallowed the cheap blend, and slumped into the nearest Chesterfield. Where to start looking?

Gina ushered everyone into the drawing room, now set up for coffee and drinks, which were laid out on the mahogany sideboard. Mali wandered in with the others and was impressed by Gina's ability to easily defuse the tension that had been building over dinner. A change of room, seating position and strong coffee would probably make all the difference. Not everyone had the same idea, though. Harrison and Madeleine immediately gravitated to the corner of the drawing room and sat, once again, close together, not inviting any small talk from anyone else. Maybe rude, maybe just wary, thought Mali, especially after watching the dreadful behaviour of Jeremy towards Madeline over dinner, as well as his rudeness about the food. He hadn't mellowed since the Q&A session. *Looks like a man with a permanent grudge*, thought Mali, *you can see it in his face, sort of pinched and mean.*

She sat down near Pippa and Oscar, who seemed to be totally absorbed in their own conversation. She was lost in her own thoughts about the retreat when she overheard them mention this Codex Pippa had spoken of earlier. They seemed to lower their voices when they did but Mali still caught a few details and was intrigued. Her grandparents had talked about a missing Codex more than once and Owain always thought it might be buried treasure. She could still see all the excitement and intrigue in Owain's young face when he talked about mysteries and secrets. Thirteen years without him seemed like a lifetime.

Wary of being overheard, Pippa and Oscar's conversation had moved on to a possible art exhibition at Ravenshade Manor.

That would be good for Ravenshade, Mali mused, and maybe a story for Pippa to cover. Oscar's demeanour and knowledge gave the impression he would know a few influential people in the art world. That could bring in some cash for a few running repairs thought Mali. Ravenshade Manor certainly looked lived in, almost shabby in places. She thought of her farmhouse and the light that filled the rooms from the new French doors and sky lights. Home seemed like days ago, not just this morning. She turned and leaned towards Oscar and Pippa.

"Sorry for interrupting but I couldn't help overhear your conversation. Impossible not to, sitting here," she smiled, by way of an explanation. "What is a Codex? I always thought it was something made up for children's mystery stories or adventure films."

Oscar and Pippa exchanged glances, and both started to respond at the same time.

"Sorry Pippa," said Oscar. "Perhaps I can explain? So, Mali, a Codex is an ancient manuscript. You may have heard of the Mayan Codex? They provide one of the few written records of Mayan culture. Fascinating. But also, one went missing in Cambridge quite some time ago now. Nothing really more to say on that." His voice trailed off, at a warning glance from Pippa.

"Oscar is going to organise an art exhibition hosted here at Ravenshade," announced Pippa. "What do you think of that, Mali? Great idea, don't you think? Showcase local and national artists. Do you paint?"

"Sadly not, I don't have much time for that I'm afraid, not with running my farm. Sorry again for interrupting. I look forward to more details about your exhibition, Oscar. Oh yes, and the Codex."

Mali sat back in her chair. That was interesting. What were those two up to? Maybe just having a good time. She was making too much of it all and it was too easy to think everyone else was there with ulterior motives, just because she was. She needed to concentrate on her own reasons for being there, to speak with Jeremy about her brother. She had to focus on finding any opportunity she could.

Mali turned to find Gina by her side. "Can I get you a drink, Mali?"

"No thank you Gina, no drink for me. It's been a long day. Great meal by the way. Thank you."

"You're welcome," Gina smiled. "The kitchen is small, but we make it work. Good idea, keeping a clear head. Long day tomorrow. Let me know if you change your mind about that drink though." She glided away, the perfect hostess, already checking to see if more coffee or something stronger was needed.

Mali turned to say goodnight to the others, but Pippa and Oscar were back to talking intently and barely seemed to notice her. Madeline and Harrison remained huddled in the corner. Vivienne and Alistair were very likely still outside trying to light wet cigarettes. She raised her hand in a sort of half-hearted farewell gesture and quietly left the room without disturbing anyone. Jeremy had said he was going to the library and this might be her only chance.

The hall was quiet apart from the storm making a valiant effort to find its way in. Now was the time, perhaps just a few minutes, to go unnoticed upstairs to Jeremy's room. A thought had formed in her mind – Jeremy had talked about his diaries, writing from memories, well what if he had some of his here, with him? All she wanted was to find his notes or diary from that dreadful year she lost her brother, or anything that might suggest he had met her brother. Owain's death had never been resolved but Mali was convinced that Jeremy knew something about it. She was ready to confront him if that was the case.

She walked slowly up the stairs, dreading any creaks from the old wood treads which might give her away. She had seen Jeremy come out of his room earlier when she was looking for her own and she headed straight for his bedroom door.

Just as Mali was nearing the top of the stairs, Gina was leaving the drawing room, heading to the kitchen to refill the coffee pot. Something caught her eye, and she saw Mali rather furtively heading for the top of the stairs. *Now where is she sneaking off to?* she wondered. *She needs to mind that creaky top step.*

Mali tentatively knocked on Jeremy's door, listened, and, content that there was no sound other than the wind outside, she slowly opened it. Silence. Just a table lamp left on, its light pooling on the floor by the desk. "He's probably scared of the dark," she muttered quietly to herself as she looked around the room. There was an opened whisky bottle and empty glass on one of the bedside tables. By the window she could see a small suitcase opened with a shirt folded on top, a hairbrush on the dressing table, and a bottle of aftershave. She walked round the bed. A jacket looked like it had been thrown on the floor but next to it was an old leather holdall. She carefully put her hands on the well-worn leather. Could she be so lucky? Her hands were shaking. What if the zip got stuck or it made a noise? She held her breath and hesitated for a moment before opening the zip. It was open and, just as she had hoped, it was full of old notebooks, scribblings by date with place names of where he had visited. She listened. There was still no sound just her heart racing. She could not believe her luck. Why carry them around with him? Probably for the much lauded, precious memoir he kept mentioning earlier. She quickly riffled through the notebooks, looking for the year 2012. Yes, here it was; an old exercise book filled with pages of notes from the year of her brother's school creative writing weekend. She felt her stomach knot and started to feel tearful. What to do now? Perhaps she should leave well alone.

Was that a sound from the corridor? Without thinking any further, she quickly ripped out the relevant pages, trying to be neat about it but failing. She packed everything back in the holdall, zipped it up, and put it back roughly where she had found it. She put her ear to the door and listened. Nothing. Gently, she opened the door and stepped quietly out in to the corridor. Thank goodness the coast was clear.

Mali failed to see Gina in the hallway below. Gina however, did not fail to spot her, leaving Jeremy's room, looking around furtively and tucking something that looked like papers, into her pocket. *Now what is she up to?* Gina wondered to herself.

Mali went quickly to her room, closing the door behind her with a huge sigh of relief and the precious pages in her pocket.

She placed them at the bottom of her suitcase. Her heart was pounding in her chest. *I can always put them back, no problem. Act normal,* she told herself. *Breathe.*

Mali turned, walked out of the bedroom door, and headed back downstairs to take Gina up on her offer of another drink.

CHAPTER 10

Ensconced in the old hunt room, the rain and wind lashing outside, Alistair had been able to finally relax.

It was an unusual room, nestled between the house and the stable block; a relic from a bygone era. The high ceiling was suspended by imposing oak beams, adorned with a central chandelier made from antlers. The flagstone floors complemented the wood-panelled walls, the upper portions of which were covered in antique peeling green paint. Above the picture rail, taxidermy trophies – once vibrant creatures – now gazed lifelessly. Long-abandoned gun cabinets lined one wall, leading to an imposing stone fireplace, where two tired green leather armchairs sat, heavy tartan blankets draped over them. The table placed between them held a Tantalus and heavy crystal glasses. It was as if past occupants had just left the room for dinner.

The one window framed the storm. Vivienne lit two pillar candles on the table between them as they sat down, shadows flickering across the floor and walls, the stag's horns seeming to grow in the light.

Alistair didn't like the taxidermy. He found it unsettling, distasteful, and, like his friend, detested hunting. He knew Vivienne planned to renovate the room for creative workshops and exhibitions. He inwardly smiled as his eye caught the white sheet draped over what he knew to be a giraffe's head. Well, Vivienne was always resourceful.

Having offered Vivienne a cigarette and, holding his lighter for her before lighting his own, he inhaled deeply: "Well Jeremy is still a piece of work isn't he, Vivienne? Obnoxious, jumped-up shit."

"He is. God only knows what we all found so attractive about him."

"I know, it makes me cringe!" He shuddered to emphasise his point. "It's a wonder Gina didn't smash the plate over his head with his arrogant complaining at dinner, which by the way was superb. She does a good job, doesn't she? Nice with it too." He had seen Gina a number of times over the years and was always impressed with her attention to detail and her un-flustered way of doing things.

"Mmm... she does," Vivienne replied, her gaze lingering on the tendrils of cigarette smoke as they rose to the roof space.

"Did you see the way he was with Mali?" he inquired. "All charm and smarm. Knowing him, he will be trying to hit on her before the night's over! We need to keep an eye on him. She seems nice, very bright, but you know how he can draw people in who don't know him."

There was a pause.

"Mmm, yes... yes we do."

Alistair tilted his head and observed his friend. It wasn't like her to not relish compliments for Gina, of whom he knew she was very fond. He had also observed her build an easy rapport with Mali. Her normal instinct would be protective.

"You ok, Vivienne? You seem a bit distracted," Alistair spoke with some concern.

"To be honest, not really. I was at William and Ruth's weekend gathering last month, Jeremy was there too. You know I see him from time to time, but I've only invited him here once, soon after I inherited the place. He was so obnoxious, never again… until now, obviously. Anyway, at William and Ruth's, he was talking about writing his autobiography and was holed up in the study, scribbling away whenever there was any free time. On Sunday morning, Jeremy and William went off riding and I'm afraid my curiosity got the better of me. I went into the study and there was the draft copy of his memoir right there on the desk. I know I shouldn't have looked, but I saw my name and couldn't resist. What I read made me feel sick. He was writing about our past relationship, but it was all lies! He distorted the facts and made me look… well… promiscuous. Said I was a tart, slept around; you know how he twists things."

"I know that he's doing his autobiography in an attempt to revive his reputation as a decent author… one final exposé and all that. But if he thinks he can tarnish my name with his pen he's got another think coming. I can't tell you how it makes my blood boil!" Vivienne off-loaded with a sense of relief in her voice, Alistair shaking his head in disbelief.

Vivienne went on, asking, "Do you remember that summer of 1979 when I first met Jeremy, you and the old crowd at the Cambridge Folk Festival?"

Alistair nodded wistfully, "We had such a wild time back then with all the parties, punting on the river, drinking and evenings spent putting the world to right into the early hours." He smiled at the memories.

"So," Vivienne continued, "can you remember me being anything other than amicable with Jeremy after we split up? I know it's never pleasant to feel rejected, but I was thoughtful about his feelings and still included him in invitations, even though I found him pompous and egotistical."

Alistair agreed and remarked that he remembered how considerate Vivienne had always been and didn't recall any particularly bad feelings. In fact, Jeremy seemed to quickly move on to other conquests!

"It probably dented his inflated ego though, you binning him off!" he chuckled. "But no, you were always too good for him; too fair and caring; far too beautiful, darling. He didn't deserve you."

Whilst the ferocious storm continued to rage outside, they lit another cigarette and explored the loathsome character that was Jeremy. How he managed to appear charming and enigmatic, casting his spell on those around him, reeling them in, using them for his own satisfaction then discarding them without a care.

"There's something else," Vivienne said. "In that rubbish he's writing, he says I shouldn't have the manor, that it's rightfully his, the family seat. I'm not the right sort of person to preserve this place for future generations. It's very clever – he's destroyed my character and then implies he only wants the place to preserve its history." Vivienne's cigarette shook a little in her fingers.

"What?" Alistair looked shocked. "But it's yours, it's

your home, you love the place, why would it belong to him?"

Until recently, she hadn't thought about all this for a very long time. She hesitated, then said, her voice brittle, "Jeremy thinks Ravenshade should have remained with the Pendleton family name. As you know, the previous owner, Charles Pendleton left the Manor to me – I'm his illegitimate daughter. I didn't know until he had died, my Mum had always told me she didn't know who my father was. Oh, you know all this…" She trailed off.

"I do, but you need to vent and I love to hear you talk, darling. Go on."

Vivienne looked at her old friend gratefully. "This happened when I was aged twenty-eight, and I can tell you, no-one was more surprised than me. Can you imagine, twenty-something liberal-minded me with a dislike of the landed gentry! I wasn't at all interested in the stately pile dripping with wealth. I didn't want to be tarred with that aristocratic brush. But when I heard it was home to the 'Old Boys Shooting Club' and the grounds were being used for hunting and shooting parties, I decided to take it on to protect the wildlife here.

"Before Ravenshade, I found the need to move on as and when the mood took me. I led a roaming, unfettered life. Through transforming these grounds into an eco-friendly haven for wildlife and tending my vegetables and herbs, I have found contentment. I enjoy the rhythm of the seasons of nature. It's the only thing that grounds me. I adore this place; being here with Gina, living my best life. And yes, it's very much my home." Vivienne's voice was strong now, full of passion.

"I love the place too, Viv. Between your passion and

Gina's practicality, you've done a great job, maintaining its character, injecting some flair." He smiled at her.

"My father Charles Pendleton made it crystal clear that he left the family estate to me to prevent it going to his younger brother's son, our very own Jeremy, who he apparently didn't like or trust. Obviously, a fine judge of character!"

There was a fierce nod of agreement from Alistair.

"The fact that I kept my mother's name Henderson and didn't take the Pendleton name is irrelevant. I still have a biological link, and anyway, it's all in a legal document."

Alistair tried to allay her fears, keeping his voice even to hide his rage, "Let's see what happens, but I'm here if you need me. Don't sit on this too long, Vivienne. I have a very good friend who is a lawyer. We can ask him to do some preliminary inquiries?"

Vivienne smiled and patted him on the shoulder, "Thanks Ali, I'm fine. I'm sure I have a way to sort it; but I appreciate the offer of your friend's help. Right, we had best make our way back, they will wonder where we are." She gave herself a little shake and stood up.

He smiled, giving her a quick hug before putting out his cigarette. "Always here for you. Right, ready to brave the storm then?" It was only a short run, but they would get soaked.

"You go on up Ali, I just want to check on the camper van."

He raised his brows. "Really Vivienne, now? In this?" She nodded and he sighed. "Alright then, but I'm coming with you."

She held up her hand and shook her head. "No Ali, I can look after myself, I won't be long." After a short debate, he gave in and reluctantly made his way back to the manor.

The rumble of thunder reverberated ominously behind Alistair as he dashed back to the house, lightning illuminating the creaking branches of the trees, the wind whipping icy pellets of rain into his face. The storm had arrived with a vengeance.

Wrestling against the wind, he had to use his shoulder to slam the heavy front door shut. He stood and shook the water from his head and jacket, still mulling over the conversation with Vivienne. He wished she had let him go with her to the van, he was uneasy about letting her go alone but knew her well enough that a no meant no. With a final shake, he hung his jacket and headed towards the drawing room and warmth.

Jeremy heard a door slam and reluctantly stopped his search of the library to check he was not about to be disturbed. As he opened the door of the library he saw Alistair in the hallway, dripping rainwater.

"Oh, it's you," he drawled, leaning against the doorway of the library, a glass cradled in his hand. "Still selling tatty old books, Fradley?" Jeremy swirled the amber liquid around the glass, a disingenuous smile on his face.

Immediately, Alistair had felt his hackles rise. "Still penning drivel, Pendleton?" he retorted. "Tell me how is it going, being a failing writer? You know it really makes me wonder where that first novel came from, was it really all yours?" Alistair knew he had hit the mark by the stiffening of Jeremy's shoulders. Good! He turned, determined to end the conversation there.

"How is that delicious little sister of yours?" Jeremy called after him. "What was her name? Ahh yes… Meg? What a delicate little beauty she was, so naive." The tone was taunting.

In a flash Alistair had turned on his heels and was standing toe to toe with Jeremy. "Don't you ever, ever speak her name again, you filthy piece of trash." Each word was punctuated with a stab of his finger into Jeremy's chest. "One of these days you will get what is coming to you, Pendleton, and I hope it's long, painful and lonely, you odious shit."

Jeremy looked a little flustered at the aggression but tried to brush it off with a nonchalant shrug. "God forgives those that repent, Alistair, you should know that." He smirked as he turned and sauntered back into the library.

Alistair stood frozen, breathing heavily, heart beating, his pulse echoing erratically in his ears. He gripped his shaking hands into two tight fists, flexing and un-flexing his fingers, watching Jeremy's back disappear through the library door.

Raking his fingers through his wet hair and down his face, he tried unsuccessfully to compose himself. He paced the darkened hallway, breathing heavily, before he made his way slowly to the drawing room. God, he badly needed a drink. Trembling hands on the door, he pinned a relaxed smile on his face and stepped into the room.

CHAPTER 11

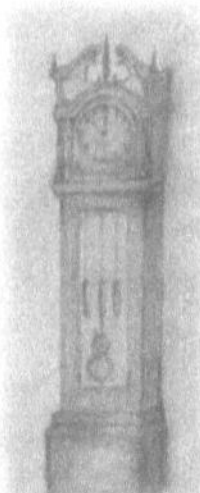

The wine had flowed; the conversations ranged from stilted to gregarious, and the storm raged like a howling banshee beyond the ancient windowpanes of the drawing room.

Harrison and Madeline were on edge. The conversations around them added to the sense of unease between them. They desperately needed to speak to Jeremy, to make some sense of everything they had found out.

"Why don't we just confront him?" said Madeline in hushed tones.

Harrison thought for a moment then grabbed Madeline's arm and whispered, "Follow me,"

"Long day, we're off to bed," he announced abruptly to the room in general.

"Where are we going?"

"To find Jeremy," replied Harrison and steered his wife towards the library. She could hardly keep up, her shoes were too high, and she stopped him still with a sharp,

"Wait! Are you sure you want to do this?" They stared at each other for a few moments.

"Yes," he replied firmly. Madeline part ran, part stumbled, to keep up with him, as a hundred squirrels ran feral in her mind in the moments before they entered the library. The grandfather clock chimed, declaring 9.45pm – making them both jump.

Harrison wiped his clammy palms on his trousers and knocked at the open door.

"I'm not here!" shouted Jeremy, in response.

"It's Harrison. Harrison and Madeline Chester, we need a word with you. We won't keep you long."

They heard what sounded like a few mumbled profanities before Jeremy replied, "You have five minutes!"

They entered the library and closed the door behind them. Jeremy was seated behind a vast leather-topped desk, topped with several huge, leather books, an ancient-looking Bakelite telephone, and an ugly-looking bronze paperweight, shaped like a rat nibbling a nut.

Harrison strode towards him, pulling a sheaf of papers from inside his jacket. "I've just been sent these," he began, his voice tight. "And I want to know, are they real?"

Jeremy raised his eyebrows, a bored expression on his face.

Harrison took a sheet of paper from the top of the pile and dropped it onto the desk in front of the other man. "My adoption certificate – with you named as my father."

He plucked a second document and dropped it on the desk, "A letter from you."

He lifted a thicker pile of documents now and threw them onto the pile, "Documents pertaining to my claim to this place, to Ravenshade Manor. The documents, the letter… are they genuine? Is it true?"

There was a long pause as the men glared at each other. Frustration and anger surged in Harrison's face, barely contained, as he waited for a response.

Jeremy sat in silence for a long moment, eyes fixed on the papers on the desk. Then he stood and came around the desk in front of Harrison, gave a small nod, and began to speak.

"The certificate. Yes, I am your father. I never denied it to myself." There was no hesitation. No attempt to explain or soften the truth. "Your mother – your adoptive mother – wrote to me. She had found my name, some carelessness on the part of the agency." Jeremy waved a hand dismissively. "I wrote back to her, saying I wanted no part of it – your birth mother was so tiresome about the whole thing, wanted us to be together, had some kind of breakdown, I believe. I know nothing of your inheritance claim, I suggest you engage a lawyer and get in the queue."

Harrison stood frozen, the weight of Jeremy's words sinking in slowly, like ink bleeding into paper. His brain was working slowly, struggling to process too much new information. This man, this odious man, really was his father. Harrison reeled, struggling to comprehend the man's coldness, his brutal words .

Jeremy stepped back and turned to face the fireplace, taking the documents and letter with him. The light from the dying flames flickered across his silhouette, which in the darkness gave him an ethereal appearance, reminiscent of a scene from Dante's Inferno.

What followed came not in a sudden burst but like a storm long gathering on the horizon, inevitable and thunderous. The clash of betrayal and disbelief, of love strained and loyalty shattered, gave what came next a brutal, undeniable force.

They watched and waited in anticipation, then slowly his shoulders began to shake. *He's crying,* thought Madeline, but then they heard him laugh. She groaned in disbelief and misery. In his last act of defiance towards this turmoiled pair, he raised his arm, about to throw the evidence onto the fire. Harrison's rage got the better of him.

Everything happened so quickly. The heated verbal exchange. The years of knowing and keeping secrets, and the years of not knowing and being kept in the dark. Decades of resentment and the shock of new knowledge, spilling over into anger, rage, and the heat of the moment. At the breaking point, time seemed to fracture, every detail thrown into sharp relief by the shifting firelight. Madeline watched her husband unravel before her eyes, the revelations of the last few hours and this man's cold indifference robbing her husband of his usual composure.

Harrison lunged first, followed in a heartbeat by Madeline. They moved with desperate precision, arms outstretched, eyes locked on the documents, their aim to salvage the evidence of Harrison's link to his past. Or at least that's what they would later claim.

They all fell together, a tangled threesome. Madeline

clutching the evidence with one hand, legs tangled with –
well she wasn't sure whose limbs. Harrison landed hard
squarely on top of Jeremy. Jeremy was still. The room fell
into an eerie, suspended silence. Jeremy had landed
forwards on the fender with a sickening crunch, his
forehead striking the metal before his body crumpled,
finally coming to rest face-down on the hearth.

Madeline scrambled backwards across the floor, her
breath stifling a scream. Harrison rolled off Jeremy's
motionless form, his chest heaving, and instinctively
backed away, snatching up the spilled papers, before
spying his wife, curled on the floor.

Harrison crouched beside her and said more gently,
"We have to go. Now! Hold on to me." He pulled her
from the room, out into the draughty hallway.

Harrison caught a glimpse of Vivienne standing in the
hallway, but it didn't seem like she had seen him. The
grandfather clock chimed the hour, its hollow tone
cutting through the stillness.

Only when they were in the privacy of their own
bedroom did the silence break.

"Oh my God Harrison, what have we done?"

Madeline crumpled to the floor, inconsolable.

CHAPTER 12

The rain came down in sheets, hammering the windshield so hard it sounded more like gravel. Detective Inspector Dougie Stevenson squinted through the blur of wipers, the world outside his car little more than shadows and flashes of headlights. Beside him, Detective Sergeant Ellie Ford was silent, arms folded, watching the storm with a tired, weary expression.

"Bloody October," Ellie muttered, as Stevenson eased the car around a tight bend in the country lane. "You'd think we'd get a break after the week we've had."

Dougie nodded. The trees lining the narrow road groaned and bent under the wind's fury. Branches scraped at the roof like desperate fingers. A massive oak loomed ahead, its trunk wide and gnarled, roots knotted into the embankment. They passed it in silence and then CRACK. A thunderous snap split the air, followed by a sickening thud. Dougie slammed on the brakes as the rearview mirror showed the tree crashing down, splitting the road where they had driven moments before. Mud and bark exploded upward like a detonated bomb.

Ellie stared back, her face pale in the dim dashboard glow. "Shit, that was close. A few seconds earlier, that would have crushed us."

"Yeah," Dougie said, his voice quiet. "Too damn close."

For a moment, neither moved. The rain softened slightly, a sudden hush in the chaos. "Better call it in, Ellie. Let the station know what has happened." After Ellie had spoken to the desk sergeant back at Parkside, Dougie exhaled and put the car back into gear. "Let's get you home." They drove on, between fallen branches scattered on the road, both silent as Dougie concentrated. Ahead, the road lay treacherous and uncertain.

They had driven less than a mile when Stevenson's phone buzzed in its cradle. The screen lit up with the duty inspector's name. Dougie answered on speaker, eyes still on the wet tarmac, "Ward?"

"Dougie, sorry to dump this on you," came the voice, tight with urgency. "We've had a 999 call, an assault at Ravenshade Manor. Caller's a man, panicked. Says he has been attacked, and that he is fearful for his life. Then the line went dead."

Dougie's grip tightened on the wheel. "Where?"

"Ravenshade Manor. It is just off the B Road, halfway to Ellie's place. We've no units anywhere close, and with the storm, and trees going down all over the place, no-one is getting through for a while. We need you to divert, check it out."

Dougie glanced at Ellie. "Understood."

"Be careful," Ward added. "Storm's knocked half the county sideways. Don't take any risks." The call ended.

When Dougie saw the sign for Ravenshade he flicked the indicator and turned onto a narrow lane leading towards the manor. The road was even worse here, flooded in places and lined with trees that bowed in the gale like mourners. One of them toppled towards them as they drove past it; the trunk was at least fifty feet away, but they felt the steering sway as, thankfully smaller, branches scraped the rear window and boot. Ellie squealed, "Bloody hell Dougie, not another one! Stop the car. I need to get out!" She grabbed at the door handle but Dougie, anticipating her panic, quickly leaned across and pulled her hand away. He drew the car to a halt, "Don't be daft Ellie. You're safer in here. We can't go back now. We'll get to the house in a few minutes. Ravenshade Manor will have weathered worse than this."

He moved off again, silently thankful that the car still had four wheels and could move. Beside him, Ellie squeezed her eyes tightly shut and muttered prayers to a god she didn't believe in, under her breath.

At last, the looming silhouette of the manor house came into view; a grand, imposing structure of limestone, dark mullioned windows foreboding in the thunderstorm.

CHAPTER 13

The clock in the hallway struck the quarter-hour. *Thank God*, thought Gina, *10.15. Surely they won't stay up much longer. My feet are killing me, I shouldn't have worn heels.* "Vanity, thy name is woman," she smiled to herself.

She liked the hallway. It always made her feel like she was living in the past. She clicked across its flagstone floor, covered in places by faded Persian rugs, considering who else may have crossed this floor over the past two centuries or more and admiring its intricate pattern, now only dimly illuminated by the embers of a fire still burning in the grate. She stooped to add a couple more logs and shadows loomed around the walls as the light flared.

To the right was the staircase. She had polished the wooden handrail to a deep shine this morning and wondered how many women had done so before her. She passed the library, its door ajar, light pooling onto the floor. Jeremy was still in there and she wasn't about to disturb him. She continued on towards the drawing room and hoisted a smile onto her face, before pushing the door open.

As Gina began to collect the used coffee cups and glasses from around the room, Pippa came towards her, stretching and yawning decorously.

"More coffee?" Gina asked.

"No, not for me, I am off to bed. That's enough excitement for me for one day." She leaned in towards Gina, dropping her voice. "A lot of big emotions around here tonight, and one giant ego!"

"You can say that again," said Gina. "Bed is probably a good idea, it's going to be a busy day tomorrow. Sleep well," she called after Pippa, who was already heading out of the door.

The drawing room was smaller than the hall, and cosier, with squashy armchairs, couches and a roaring fire. Soft light glowed from the wall sconces. The four remaining people in the room were gathered round a low coffee table at the far end of the room. Alistair's voice had become even louder since Gina had last seen him, his face an unhealthy shade of mottled red and eyes struggling to focus. He had a brandy glass in his hand and was jabbing it towards Mali to emphasise his point. She shrank backwards; not in alarm, thought Gina, but to protect that cashmere sweater.

"I am telling yooo, the Tarot never lies. Two of swords – decisions – a call to action, we have all the informashun we need, need, need – need action now."

He slumped back on the couch, resting his head on Vivienne's shoulder.

Vivienne caught Gina's eye. "I think some more coffee would be good, Gina. Maybe some water too please."

"Not sure I set much store by Tarot, crystals, that kind of thing… not sure if it's scary, or mumbo jumbo," Oscar murmured to Mali.

Gina said, "Coffee coming right up, would anyone like—"

Oscar protested, "I'm sure we can make our own coffee," he had noticed how tired Gina looked. and she had removed her apron, clearly ready for the evening to be over.

Gina smiled at him gratefully, "It's no probl…"

The words faded as the lights in the room flickered feebly a couple of times and went out.

The room was not completely dark; the fire still gave a faint glow but Gina could no longer see the faces of the other people in the room. They were just darker outlines in the gloom. She fumbled in her pocket for her phone and turned on its torch. She walked towards the group on the couches. "Not to worry. The power often trips; the fuse board is ancient…" she trailed off, cursing herself for alluding to the house's poor state of repair, which she and Vivienne had been at such pains to disguise.

There was a movement on one of the couches and a looming, dark shape revealed itself as Oscar, in the beam of Gina's torch. Another light flared as he too turned on his phone's torch.

"Could be the storm has knocked out the power," he said.

"You are probably right," Gina answered gratefully. "I'll go and check the fuse board just in case. It's in the kitchen and there's plenty of candles and matches there too, and a couple of torches."

"I'll come and help," offered Oscar easily and Gina

thought again what a gentleman he was.

"Won't be a tick," she offered to the dark, seated shapes. She held the phone up towards them and Vivienne and Mali smiled. Alistair's head was still on Vivienne's shoulder. He was fast asleep.

CHAPTER 14

Pippa had left the drawing room at precisely 10:15, just as the grandfather clock struck the quarter-hour, its delicate tinkle of sound a contrast to the gathering noise of the storm outside. The evening had been anything but dull; she had spent a lively and engaging evening in conversation with Alistair and Oscar, both men clearly captivated by the mystery surrounding the Mayan Codex and how it may have come to be at Ravenshade Manor. Pippa loved nothing more than discussing intrigue and with people who had intellectual energy.

Pippa had revealed her working theory, confident now in its clarity that Alfred Pendleton had stolen the Codex in 1946 and brought it to his brother's ancestral home, hiding it somewhere within the manor, most likely in the library. To her surprise, Alistair had more than a polite interest; it turned out he had his own suspicions and a few clues of his own. Pippa had been particularly intrigued by Alistair's quiet whispering that Alfred Pendleton was, in fact, Jeremy Pendleton's father. She knew that from her research, of course, but she felt sure that was why Jeremy was here too, and not to return the Codex to the university library, but to find it for his own ends. Well, with the help of Alistair and Oscar, she would get there first. The pieces were beginning to fall into place.

Having said her goodnights to the others in the drawing room, Pippa quietly made her way towards the library, the Persian rugs in the hallway muting her footsteps. The lights flickered intermittently as the storm continued to surge against the walls of the manor. The heavy oak door to the library stood closed, a sliver of light seeping out from beneath it. She hesitated. Was someone inside?

She knocked once, then again. Silence.

Her curiosity, always a force stronger than fear, compelled her forward. She pushed the door open slowly and stepped inside.

The library greeted her like a sleeping beast, vast and quiet. The room was hushed and still, the fire reduced to a dull glow of coals. Books towered in the shelves, the spines catching the flickering light. Outside, the storm continued to lash against the windows, rain rattling like stones on glass. She fumbled for the light switch and the wall lights illuminated the room.

Near the large desk sat a high-backed, buttoned leather armchair, bold and imposing in the quiet gloom. Seated in it was Jeremy Pendleton, a figure of solemn stillness. At first glance, he looked lost in thought.

Pippa froze. The sight of him there startled her.

"Mr Pendleton, are you all right?" she asked cautiously, her voice low as she stepped closer.

He didn't respond. The silence deepened in the room. Something was wrong.

Stepping closer, the hairs now on her neck rising and a creeping sense of dread crawling into her chest.

"Mr Pendleton?" she tried again, concern growing. "Are you unwell?"

She moved to stand directly before him and the truth became painfully clear. Jeremy Pendleton was dead, his eyes open, stared seeing nothing. The stillness of the body wasn't thoughtful, it was absolute. Lifeless.

A single ribbon of blood trickled down his forehead, slow and surreal, like a feather drifting from the branch of a tree. It was a moment suspended in time: silent, solemn, and utterly final. Pippa stared, frozen in disbelief. Then the lights went out.

The room was swallowed by darkness and the framed silhouette of the body in the chair took on an eerie, almost unreal quality, ghostly and still. Only the pale outlines of the furniture and the man in the chair were visible. A jolt of panic surged through her. She screamed. The sound echoed off the stone and wood, ringing down the corridors of Ravenshade Manor like a warning bell in the night.

The immediate blackness, had plunged every room into shadow. Gina and Oscar had headed off to find candles and torches from the kitchen. In the drawing room the fire snapped and popped, throwing distorted silhouettes across the walls. Vivienne, Alistair and Mali fearfully peered through the darkened room at each other, frozen in mid-conversation, their eyes adjusting in the dim flicker of light from the fire.

The scream, combined with the raging wind and rain, hauntingly echoed in the space.

"What is going on? Alistair, Mali, stick together," gasped Vivienne, reaching for their hands, voice taut.

As they entered the hallway, Gina and Oscar appeared with candles and torches. The beams of light jittered across the darkened hallway. For a moment they were horrified at the sight of a bear looming along the wall, before their eyes adjusted. It was just the eerie shadow cast by the black forest bear umbrella stand, against the autumnal leaves from the urn on the console table towering up the walls, like a grisly shadow puppet theatre. They all took a deep breath and looked around.

The violent storm outside sent howling sounds rattling through the bones of the tired old place and they had to speak loudly to hear each other.

"Where did the scream come from?" asked Gina, her candle flickering as the draughts flitted around the hallway.

"I'm not sure." Vivienne said, appearing in the hall, still clutching Alistair's and Mali's hands. She cast a worried glance toward Gina.

"Could it be Pippa? She just left to go to bed…" Mali said anxiously.

Alistair now feeling like he needed to sober up added, "Pippa – she may have fallen when the lights went off?"

"It sounded closer, not from upstairs… maybe the library?" said Oscar. "I wonder if the storm has ripped through a window and broken something."

Vivienne turned to speak but a sudden pounding on the

front door silenced her. Everyone froze. Then it came again, the heavy door knocker deliberate and sombre against the oak. They all stood motionless as the darkness tightened around them.

CHAPTER 15

Abandoning the car in front of the manor, the two detectives hurried towards a stone porch which sheltered a carved oak door. It also shielded them from another onslaught of torrential rain. Ellie banged an iron door knocker in the shape of a raven against the door and they waited.

"Try again," Dougie urged and Ellie banged on the door knocker with more force this time. After a few moments, they heard a heavy bolt being drawn from the inside and the door opened a couple of inches. A tall woman peered out, her face ghostly in the gloom.

"Detective Inspector Dougie Stevenson. Can we come in, madam?" Dougie said, shoving his warrant card into the gap.

The woman opened the oak door of Ravenshade Manor and allowed the detective and his partner to enter. The door slammed shut and the woman stepped in front of them, looking terrified by this turn of events. Stevenson's sharp eyes swept over the flag-stoned entrance hall. Warm embers and flames glowed from a fire in a marble hearth but did little to dispel the heavy air of unease. The glow illuminated a small crowd of people; they all seemed shocked at the sight of them. He wondered what they were all doing in the hall.

Sergeant Ellie Ford had the measure of the gathering in seconds: posh, arty-farty types, too much booze, too few real-life problems, minor skirmish over seating arrangements and, 'Let's call out PC Plod to sort it out.' Dougie scanned each person, trying to read their faces for fear, or guilt, which might be hiding in plain sight. In their confusion, they all started to talk at once.

Dougie held up his hands and, raising his voice, called, "Quiet!"

The commotion ceased immediately, as if a stern teacher had called an unruly class to order.

"We received a call to say an assault has taken place, and we would like to speak to the person who made that call," Ellie stated loudly.

The woman who had opened the door stepped towards the detectives. Multiple strings of coloured beads adorned her neck and she fingered them nervously, as though they were a rosary. She wore a vivid blue floating dress with a weirdly uneven hem. Silver jewellery adorned her neck, wrists and ears, and long grey hair fell almost to her waist. *An obvious hippie by the look of her*, thought Ellie.

"And you are?" Ellie asked, nodding her head in the woman's direction while retrieving her notebook from her bag.

"Vivienne Henderson. I own Ravenshade Manor. We are holding a writers' retreat, and these are our guests who arrived today." She waved her arm towards the people standing behind her. "The storm has knocked all the lights out so Gina, my Estate Manager, has distributed torches and candles.”

Everyone began to fidget and talk at the same time again and, exasperated, Dougie said, “DS Ford, can you escort the rest of these people to…’ He trailed off, looking at Vivienne. “Is there a suitable room where your guests can wait?”

“Erm, the drawing room, I suppose.” Vivienne looked at Gina for confirmation, as always.

Gina stepped forward, addressing DS Ford, “I’ll show you. Shall I also ask the Chesters to join us? They had already gone to bed before,” she hesitated, searching for the right words, “all this happened.”

The Detective Inspector cut in, “Yes, please. Is there anyone else in the house?”

Gina thought for a moment and looked at the small group of people in the hallway,

“Yes, Pippa and Jeremey Pendleton aren’t here – I thought Pippa had gone to bed, I’m not sure about Jeremy,” and gestured with her arm to a door on the left of the hallway. “It’s just through here.”

There was some muttering amongst the group, but they followed Gina and the detective sergeant meekly enough. “DS Ford, make a full list of those present – names and contact details and check who else is in the property please.”

Ellie rolled her eyes at her boss, as if to say *obviously!*

“Ms Henderson, could you tell me who made the call and who has been assaulted in your party tonight?” the inspector asked quietly, trying to regain some sense of authority.

“I have no idea, Inspector. The lights went out and

there was a scream which brought us all into the hall – we thought it was Pippa perhaps, then there was a knock on the door and, well, here you are."

Vivienne looked bemused and Dougie was beginning to feel the same, when a young woman appeared from the library, her phone torch held high and announced loudly and with a slight tremor in her voice, "He's dead? Jeremy is dead, in there, on a chair, lifeless. What the fuck is going on? Do you think I can write about this?"

"Are you Pippa?" the detective asked.

Vivienne had a look of sheer panic and bewilderment on her face, "Yes, that is Pippa. Are you all right Pippa? What's happened? Are you hurt?"

Pippa did not answer and DI Stevenson went on as if she had not spoken, "I am DI Stevenson, Cambridgeshire Police. There's been a fatality, you say?"

Pippa, ever eager to be helpful, nodded.

"Pippa, can you explain to me what's going on here?" DI Stevenson quietly requested.

"Well Detective," she began eagerly, "it must have been just after 10:15, I'd already heard the clock chime - I entered the library and there he was, dead. I thought at first he was snoozing, but he didn't answer me, so I looked at him closely and he is definitely dead." Pippa stated all this in full reporter voice. Dougie almost expected her to whip out a notepad.

"Mrs Henderson, could you join the others in the drawing room please?"

"It's Ms Henderson, actually," said Vivienne looking vaguely offended by her dismissal from the drama, but she walked off towards the drawing room, as instructed.

Dougie gestured to the door Pippa had come from,

"That's the library, I assume?"

The young woman nodded.

"Wait here please." He went into the room.

The scent of old leatherbound books and polished wood lingered in the air. And something else; a smell – metallic – met him immediately. Dougie wrinkled his nose and automatically flicked on the light switch, but nothing happened.

He reached into his pocket and brought out his phone, turning on the torch. Sweeping its beam across the room, the light caught on an armchair, with a man slumped in it. Male… late sixties, early seventies, he guessed. The head lolled unnaturally to one side and the man's face stared up at the ceiling. There was no doubt he was dead; nothing could be done for him now and he could not even get a bloody paramedic here to confirm the death, as was protocol. DI Stevenson felt fleetingly wrongfooted, without the usual procedures to anchor him.

He stepped out into the hall, motioning for Pippa to follow him as he walked towards the drawing room. As they approached the door, he asked, "Why did you so excitedly ask if you could 'write about this'?"

"Well, I am a journalist with the *Gilded Quill* in Cambridge. It's a student paper, and it isn't very often a story like this is put in front of you. It was a flippant comment, and my apologies; not really appropriate under the circumstances."

He opened the drawing room door and ushered Pippa inside. "Thank you Pippa, I'll need to talk to you again." He caught Ellie's eye and she immediately grasped that he needed her. After telling everyone to remain where they were, she headed back to the library with him.

Switching on her own phone torch, Ellie stepped into the room. The silence was oppressive.

"This is bigger than my entire flat," she said. She moved her phone around the space, taking in the scene.

Shelves crammed with books rose high into the shadows. At floor level, the fireplace glowed and sparked with the embers of a dying fire. She could see the fireplace 'thingy' – 'fender', Dougie clarified – had shifted and there was a lump of what could have been dirty sheep's wool if it had been on a barbed wire fence, only this looked darker and stickier. As she lifted her phone, the torch beam highlighted the mantelpiece lined with various colourful Chinese ceramic ornaments. She paused beside Dougie, taking in the scene. The victim lay sprawled in an oxblood leather button backed armchair. A deep cut to his forehead had caused a trail of blood to run down his face, and blood pooling beneath had dripped onto a worn Persian rug. A crystal tumbler lay nearby. Its contents had the unmistakable scent of whisky. Stevenson leaned down to the body and felt for signs of life, just to be sure, again. He shook his head when he found none.

"We need to close this room off, Ellie. Go to the car, will you, and get the crime scene tape, and the rest of the paraphernalia. We need to bag the tumbler for starters, and bring a forensic cover for the body – we need to preserve any evidence until the SOCOs can get here."

Dougie handed Ellie the car keys and she left hurriedly.

The detective walked back into the hall. He urgently needed to make a call to Parkside Police Station, but before he could, Vivienne Henderson emerged from the drawing room and walked across the hall towards him.

"All the guests are gathered in the drawing room now, obviously wanting to know what's going on. If I'm going to keep them calm, I really do need a bit more information… please!"

Dougie asked for her and the guests' continuing patience, "You've done a great job so far. You will have to trust me a little longer – I'm sorry. Now, I need to talk to Pippa Whitcombe again. Would you ask her to step out here please? I won't keep her long." Frustrated but mollified by Dougie's diplomatic response, Vivienne returned to the drawing room and Pippa stood before him a minute later.

"That must have been quite a shock you had, Pippa. How are you feeling?" he asked.

"I'm all right, not something I was expecting just before I went to bed," she said matter-of-factly.

"How come you were in the library? Was anyone else with you?" Dougie questioned.

"I was on my own, looking for a book to read." Pippa eyed the detective. He looked tired; world-weary, she thought. His crumpled jacket and crooked silk tie did nothing to dispel the illusion.

"Did you touch anything while you were in there, Pippa?" Dougie prompted gently.

Pippa hesitated. She had of course entered the library to look for clues as to where the Mayan Codex might be found. After all, it was why she was here at the manor in the first place. She was determined nothing was going to stop her from finding it. Even a dead body.

She hadn't really touched anything as it was when she had turned to search the shelves that she noticed the tutor, Jeremy Pendleton, lying slumped in the chair. And the blood. It was after she realised he was dead she did a quick reccy, all the time thinking the Codex must be there, at the same time thinking gosh what a scoop, *Body in Library of has-been Jeremy Pendleton* or *Dead in the Oxblood Chair Jeremy Pendleton a once renowned Cambridge Author*. The headlines would be delicious, she thought.

"No, I didn't touch anything," she lied, not meeting Dougie's stare. "I screamed as soon as I saw him and then made my way to the hallway, and you had arrived."

"That's helpful. Thank you, Pippa. Hmm, a journalist – not the sort that won't let the truth get in the way of a good story I trust? You can go back and join the others. I will be along shortly with my sergeant."

"Thank you. If you need any further assistance don't hesitate to ask. I haven't written about a dead body before, but I am very happy to assist you in the investigation as my strengths are uncovering mysteries," Pippa tried not to feel over-excited by the possibility she could be part of the investigation.

She went back into the drawing room. Gina, who had just sat down to take breath after rushing around with candles and torches, raised herself from the sofa.

"Pippa, would you like a drink? A little brandy or something? You've had a real shock there."

"No, no Gina, please sit down. What an evening, you must be exhausted!" Pippa seated herself on the edge of the sofa.

"I will just get everyone a drink of brandy, to settle the nerves." Gina bustled away.

Dougie finally managed to make the call to Parkside. He urgently needed an ambulance, Scene of Crime Officers (SOCO), and the medical examiner, but after he had relayed the situation to the control centre and confirmed once again the exact location of the fallen trees, he was left with no doubt that he and his DS were on their own. No help was coming. He placed his phone back in his jacket pocket and stood deep in thought. A distant rumble of thunder echoed through the house and somewhere in the manor a clock chimed.

Ellie battled her way back up the steps and into the front hall. Dougie had to open the door to let her in. She had got even wetter, and her hair was clinging to her face like tendrils of seaweed. She had the crime scene tape looped over one arm and a bag with all the investigative kit squeezed under the other. She stood dripping before her boss. Pulling her hair back, she put the bag on the floor and rummaged inside for gloves. Then she moved down the hallway to the library door and zigzagged it with the police tape. No one could accidentally fail to notice that entry had been denied.

"I've spoken to the station, Ellie. The roads are impassable – fallen trees and power down. It's chaos out there. We're on our own, at least until tomorrow."

They exchanged a grim look. *We can do this. I've got your back, and you've got mine.*

CHAPTER 16

DI Stevenson and DS Ford stood in the doorway of the drawing room, observing the guests, most of whom were seated. Vivienne Henderson and Alistair Fradley stood together by the fireplace. Mali Pritchard and Oscar Martin-Bramston sat close to Pippa Whitcombe, and Mali held Pippa's hand comfortingly.

Gina Meredith, fully back in work mode, bustled around everyone, dispensing brandy, "Good for shock," she said, as she poured herself a small amount.

The Chesters were on the edge of the group, distancing themselves. Madeline was clearly upset but declined the offer of brandy. Harrison had his arm around her shoulders. He looked pale, as though he might vomit.

"May I have your attention," DI Stevenson stepped into the room, his voice cutting through the tension like a blade. "I need you all to remain calm and listen carefully." The room fell silent. "I must inform you that Mr Jeremy Pendleton is dead and his death is being treated as suspicious. No-one is to leave the house as it is now a crime scene. I request that you all refrain from using your phones. If you do use them, it will be taken very seriously as a breach of the law in these extenuating circumstances. I cannot have anyone discussing or posting anything on social media. Is that understood?"

Pippa pulled her hands away from Mali. "You are right sir, this is a situation that needs to be kept tight. There is no power or Wi-Fi, so that will help," she added assertively, mentally noting all the titbits of information for later when she could write up her notes.

Alistair turned to DI Stevenson, "So I guess that means we're all suspects then? You think one of us had a reason to bump him off?"

Dougie was surprised to catch a glance between Alistair and Oscar. Alistair's expression had seemed almost triumphant at the news of Jeremy's demise. Oscar returned his look with a worried frown. Dougie wondered what it could mean, filing it away in his brain for the time being.

"Well good luck with that, Detective Inspector Stevenson. In terms of motive, you will be hard pressed to find anyone that liked the man." Alistair dropped himself into a chair and casually crossed his legs.

Vivienne rose to her feet, indignant. "Surely you can't think one of us…"

Dougie interrupted her firmly, "Everyone in this house is a person of interest. DS Ford is going to be conducting initial interviews shortly and I would ask for your full cooperation. In the meantime, I suggest you make yourselves comfortable. In any case, as you are aware, the weather has taken a serious turn and the storm has intensified. Local roads are blocked by fallen trees, and several power lines are reportedly down across the main routes to Ravenshade Manor. I have recently spoken with Parkside Police control unit, and backup units, forensics, and even ambulance crew have had to be diverted, or halted. None of them can get through to us for now.'

"You're saying we're stranded here?" Alistair asked. "Gina, another brandy then please."

"For the time being, yes," Dougie replied calmly. "Until the storm eases and emergency services can clear the roads, we are on our own."

Alistair scoffed. "Surely someone can make it up here with a four-wheel drive?"

Vivienne Henderson's hand trembled as she set down her glass. "But… we have a dead body in the library."

"And perhaps, a murderer in this room," said Pippa, a little too eagerly.

"I am well aware," Dougie said drily. "And that is exactly why I am insisting you stay out of the library and make yourselves available for questioning, until the storm passes and we have access to full resources."

Suddenly, Madeline Chester stood. She was shaking, and her husband pulled on her hand, encouraging her to sit down again.

"Please," he said.

"We didn't mean to kill him," Madeline said loudly. "It was an accident."

CHAPTER 17

The heavy door of the bedroom groaned shut behind DI Stevenson as he locked it from the outside. Inside, Harrison sat on the edge of a brocade-upholstered chaise, his fingers steepled under his chin, cufflinks glinting in the candlelight. The storm lashed the windows and they rattled in their frames. Despite his wife's confession, Harrison tried to retain the air of being in control, but his hair was ruffled and mildly unkempt and underneath the surface there was a deep, terrifying dread of what may come next.

The room was the one that had been allocated to the Chesters for their stay at the manor. Their half-unpacked cases lay on the floor, unzipped. There was a high coved ceiling and a four-poster bed. Perhaps this had once been a place of elegance but tonight the space felt more like a prison cell.

Harrison could hear footsteps below. Voices. The police moving from room to room, he supposed, searching for something, anything, that could untangle the mess they had all found themselves in. There was movement downstairs in the drawing room, where his wife, Madeline, was about to be questioned. What he would give for a glass of brandy now. The Inspector's plan was clear: separate them, see if their stories matched. He could still see the mingled looks of shock and surprise on everyone's faces, after his wife's confession, and squirmed: part embarrassment – he hated to be the centre of attention – and part fear.

Stevenson and Ellie stood together in the hall. "I'm starving," complained Ellie.

"Perhaps Gina will make us a sandwich; she seems helpful," said Dougie hopefully.

Ellie let go of a twist of hair to cross her fingers. "Let's hope so."

As if on cue, they saw Gina emerge from the kitchen, carrying a large coffee pot. "Coffee?" she offered and, anticipating a decent boost of caffeine, the detectives followed her into the drawing room where Madeline was sitting at a table, anxiously waiting, picking at the skin around her fingernails.

"I have made you sandwiches," Gina told the detectives. "I will leave them here. All the other guests are in their rooms now."

Dougie and Ellie thanked her and Gina disappeared back into the kitchen.

DI Stevenson steadily observed Madeline, who was crying again; a short blonde wisp of a thing in her late thirties, she obviously hadn't eaten a meaningful carbohydrate since pre-Covid.

Ellie felt nervous herself. Christ she could do with a fag but instead she pulled at an escaped strand of hair and twisted it round her finger. She remembered herself before it found its way into her mouth, unloosed the stray hair, pulled out her notebook and put her hands on the table just in time for Dougie, lead detective, to begin the interview.

"Madeline. Can I call you that?" Dougie's tone was surprisingly soft and gentle and Madeline nodded. "As we explained, we are going to record this conversation on DS Ford's phone. Do you understand? We have already talked about your rights, which you still have even in these exceptional circumstances, with particular attention to your rights to a legal representative. Can you confirm you are happy to continue without legal representation?"

"Yes," sniffed Madeline in reply.

"Why don't you start from when you and Harrison entered the library and tell me what happened?"

"We went to talk to him, about everything we'd found out…" Her voice faltered and she gestured to the documents on the table between them. "You know, the adoption certificate and the letter. It had all been such a shock for us both and we wanted to ask him about them, but, well, then it all went pear-shaped. We—"

"In what way?" interrupted DI Stevenson

"At first, he owned up to everything, I thought he was going to tell us what happened all those years ago. He looked like he was crying, but he laughed, a proper mean snigger. He had the evidence in his hand and was about to throw it in the fire. I just… it was instinctive… leapt to try to grab it, but I knocked him clean off his feet and I landed on top of him, and we must have stumbled. I was wearing those stupid heels. He hit his forehead on the fender. The thud was awful. A real crack. We knew straight away he was dead."

"How?"

"Sorry?"

"How did you know he was dead? Did you check?"

"Well, no, I, we were in shock."

"Mmm. Okay." DI Stevenson changed tack. "What time did this take place?"

"Just before 10pm I think – yes it was because as we left the library, that grandfather clock chimed 10 o'clock."

"Did you see anyone else, Madeline?"

"No, I don't think so."

DI Stevenson refocused his thoughts. Both detectives noticed Madeline was stimming; her right leg was jigging, and three fingers of her left hand were playing a beat so fast against her leg it looked like she was plugged in. *Definitely on the spectrum*, Dougie thought.

"Okay, Madeline. Where was Harrison while all this was going on, and why didn't he intervene to help you?" Madeline thought hard about this, and what would be the most moral and loyal response. What if Harrison's answers didn't match hers? Which they wouldn't. There really was only one response…

"No comment."

"I also need to know more about the conversation between the three of you," he pushed.

"Again, no comment."

"What did you think, boss?" Ellie asked.

"Hmmm?" Dougie was clearly lost in thought. "Let's see what the husband has to say before we start speculating."

"Fair enough," Ellie said. "I'll walk Madeline up to her room and bring Harrison down with me."

Ellie, concerned about Madeline's state of mind, thought this would provide the perfect opportunity to check on her well-being. It would also give her some time to engage in a little bit of one-to-one discussion in the hope of digging deeper and uncovering some facts which may help the case. Madeline was all over the place and her guard would be down; the best time to let secrets out.

DS Ford repeated the legalities to Harrison en route back down to the library. Harrison was extremely agitated. His tie and jacket had been removed, and he almost ran down the stairs to get to the drawing room.

"She's lying, Sergeant — to protect me!" squealed Harrison before he had even sat in the chair.

He wasn't sure he could do this. He felt cold and clammy. The thought of having to be interviewed by the police in what felt like a haunted old house, lit by candlelight, was enough to send him into a full-blown meltdown. He felt slightly nauseous and the unfamiliar surroundings were doing nothing to calm his anxious mind.

DI Stevenson turned slowly towards him. DS Ford could see Stevenson was as confident as ever and fully in control of the interview. She remembered what he had told her previously; a suspect's panic can be contained and used. No need for anxiety, she leaned forward, clasping her neatly manicured hands on the table in front of her. She was ready to hear where Dougie would take this interview. Notebook at the ready, recorder on…

"OK, Mr Chester… Harrison, if I may call you that." Ellie knew it was a rhetorical question. "Please tell me what happened in the library with Mr Pendleton," he spoke quietly, almost gently.

Harrison proceeded to tell the same account, almost identical to his wife's, until they came to the end: "He – Jeremy – Mr Pendleton, he went to put the papers on the fire, he was going to burn all the evidence, everything we have, so I went for him, landed on top of him, and his head hit that fire surround, fender thing. Madeline jumped too, but in those heels, you know, she was slower, stumbled." He raised his eyes to the detective's face, "I killed Jeremy Pendleton."

DS Ford was momentarily taken with the couple's loyalty for each other. But only momentarily. At the signal from her boss, she spread the contents of the package across the table, laying Harrison's life bare for them to see. Harrison buried his head in his hands and took a deep breath; he crumpled and wondered how in the space of 24 hours his safe, compartmentalised life had dismantled quite so quickly.

"My mother died recently." A look of confusion crossed his face. "My adoptive mother – I only found that out today – I am adopted. Jeremy Pendleton, he is – was – my father. I found that out today too."

DI Stevenson, waited patiently. He knew from experience that giving a suspect the time to speak in their own words could be just as profitable as trying to hurry things along with questions. Sure enough, Harrison began to speak again, his eyes fixed on the table.

"Francesca, my sister, she has been clearing Mum's house and digging into family history, you know… when we arrived here, there was a package from her, waiting for us. All the documents you have now seen." He gestured to the papers on the table between them. "She bought us this writing retreat supposedly as a gift – she knew Jeremy Pendleton would be here, that I would want to speak to him." He raised his eyes to the policeman's face now, "He was vile, when I asked him about it. He was so cold, dismissive, like I was nothing, like it meant nothing."

DI Stevenson looked thoughtful. "You say you were trying to save the evidence, but I think you lost your temper, that your emotions got the better of you? Understandable, you have had a terrible shock today and anyone might have done the same…" he let his statement hang in the air.

The light from the candles flickered and Harrison Chester looked quite distraught, but he replied, quick as a flash, "It was an accident – I wouldn't consider any of it a motive for murder!"

DI Stevenson wondered what Harrison would consider a motive for murder. But he kept that query in his back pocket for later.

The evidence fitted. The injury on the forehead, both accounts the same, whichever one of them, 'fell' on Jeremy, there was a clear motive, if murder was to be pursued in this case. But then there was that nagging thought at the back of DI Stevenson's head, which generally meant he was missing something. Their accounts and the position in which the body was found didn't quite make sense. Then there was the phone call. The time frame of this was becoming much more important than he had initially thought.

Having completed their interviews with both husband and wife, Dougie and Ellie agreed it was best to keep the two separated for the remainder of the evening. Tensions remained high, and the detectives needed to avoid any possibility of collusion or them cooking up a different version of events. This measure was both precautionary and procedural, allowing for reflection and discouraging any opportunity for one party to influence the other's actions or words.

Gina found rooms for both Ellie and Madeline, who was distraught all over again at being kept apart from her husband.

Dougie had opted to sleep on a large couch placed against a wall on the wide landing. It suited his needs though, and he found it was surprisingly comfortable. Also, the arrangement allowed him to remain on guard overnight, keeping an eye on both suspects.

He pondered their stories; they fitted the injury Dougie had seen on Jeremy's forehead, and the blood on the fireplace fender. Was it enough to kill the man, though? He didn't relish the thought but realised he was going to have investigate the injuries to the body more closely in daylight. It should have been the medical examiner's job, but under the circumstances Dougie had no choice but to get his hands dirty. Madeline's state of mind troubled him too. This, the horrible image which had arisen unbidden of his soon-to-be bloodied hand and the overload of caffeine kept him awake for some time, but eventually he fell into a restless sleep.

CHAPTER 18

At precisely 3 am, the grandfather clock let out a deep, resonant chime. From behind separate doors, Pippa, Alistair and Oscar emerged, silent as shadows. Their goal was to reach the library and uncover the Codex. Alistair had sent the riddle he had found to the WhatsApp group Pippa had created. She had lain in bed, reading and rereading it. Like Alistair, she was increasingly convinced that the Codex was within the library:

Find the place where two oaks meet
Look at the roots beneath their feet
Enter where the Ravens sit and caw
Through the giant's oaken door
With your back to the windows light,
    seek the colour blue
The virtuous sword will show
    the one that's true
Look at the card where less acorns fall
And find the twin upon the wall
There you will finally find
All you seek he tried to hide.

Pippa gave both Oscar and Alistair a stern look, silently urging them not to make a noise, while glancing towards the landing. Dressed in black dungarees and a striped black-and-white long-sleeved tee, Pippa looked a bit like Desperate Dan.

Sprawled on the faded chaise longue, Detective Dougie lay fast asleep, snoring softly, his limbs limp and undisturbed. His jacket was buttoned and one of the pockets revealed his phone poking out. One sound too loud and their mission would end before it began. Holding their collective breath, the trio crept onward, into the heart of the sleeping house.

They moved carefully down the back staircase, the striped carpet threadbare with age, groaning beneath each cautious step. Alistair, still flushed with brandy, struggled to contain a fit of drunken giggles.

At the library door, Pippa turned to face Alistair and Oscar, her voice low but firm. She reminded them that Jeremy's body would still be inside, untouched, unmoved.

"At no point," she said, eyes locking with theirs, "should we approach it, let alone touch it. Is that clear?"

Her gaze lingered on Alistair, her tone sharper now. Alistair blinked, sobering slightly under her scrutiny. The weight of her words settled over them like dust in the dark. Wow, she was not to be messed with.

"I don't want to go anywhere near the old bastard," Oscar whispered.

"Oscar, you'll stand guard outside. Alistair, do you understand?"

Oscar shook his head, "No, no, I am coming in, I'll stand guard, but I'm not staying out here, please just be quick, both of you."

Pippa, buzzing about the events and desperate to write about it all as soon as she got back to Cambridge, could not keep still. "Look," she said suddenly, lowering her voice and leaning in, her eyes bright with a mix of nerves and determination. "I know the Mayan Codex is here. Something about Pendleton's private collection of books is calling to me that the Codex is hidden in plain sight in that library, and also too many clues have led me here. The evening it went missing, Alfred Pendleton's alibi was shady; the fact he spent every weekend here with his brother; the fact the house was left to Vivienne in Charles' will and not his brother, and the fall-out from that legacy… my gut tells me that it is in that Library."

She glanced toward the hallway as if the inspector might be lurking there. "Charles Pendleton was obsessed with lost knowledge. Coded languages, ancient calendars, and antiquities. When the manuscript disappeared, there were rumours about his brother… and Jeremy, being Jeremy, could not help but boast that he had been told by his father it was hidden here, right here, in this library."

The heavy door to the library creaked open, the sound swallowed quickly by the thick hush within, and the tape positioned in a cross from one corner to another made Pippa pause, but only momentarily.

She slipped inside first, stepping through the tape, followed closely by Alistair and Oscar, the latter on duty now to keep the door ajar, his eyes focused on the hallway, alert. He was under strict instruction to hiss loudly if the Inspector or his sidekick Ellie came into view, or anyone else for that matter.

Alistair raised an eyebrow. "You think he was killed for the Codex?"

Pippa nodded, a bit too quickly. "I think, Harrison and Madeline knew. Or guessed. You saw how they were with Jeremy at dinner, whispering by the fire. I think they confronted him, got into an argument, and things got out of hand."

Oscar whispering, "The storm's taken down half the trees on the lane. No-one is coming or going anytime soon, so what do you think happens next, if they are the murderers?"

There was a sudden creak from somewhere deep in the house and all of them held their breath for a moment, before Oscar seemed to come to his senses, "None of that matters now. Hurry up you two, before we are caught."

"Exactly, let's get going," Pippa said, eyes gleaming. "If the Codex is here and we find it, before we leave, just imagine giving it back to the University Library, it would be wonderful." Pippa went off into Pippa's world momentarily.

The three of them fell silent, the tick-tock of the grandfather clock filling the space between them. Outside, the garden lay still, but the house felt anything but, with the wind still tempering its soul.

The room had not changed since the night before, but in the phone torch light and the eclipsed clouded moon that filtered through the tall, glassed windows, it felt altered. More foreboding. The oxblood-red leather chair still cradled Jeremy's body, now covered with a white, plastic sheet that somehow made the whole thing worse. His form was too still, too present.

Pippa tried not to look, but her eyes flicked toward the chair all the same. She swallowed hard and moved quickly to the shelves.

The library of Ravenshade Manor was famous, once meticulously curated by the enigmatic Charles Pendleton, who had passed away under his own cloud of secrets decades earlier. The shelves stretched to the ceiling, packed with books bound in leather, vellum, and faded cloth. It smelled of old woodsmoke and forgotten thoughts.

Alistair pulled a small card from his coat pocket and held it out to Pippa. "This Tarot Card is a clue," he said quietly. "Two of Swords. Look – only one acorn at the base, where the Coat of Arms has two, and see the ravens?"

The card was strange. Stark. A black bird perched at the base of the crossed swords, wings folded, watching. The missing acorn was deliberate, an omission, not a flaw. And the back of the card bore a snippet of verse in fine copperplate.

"Ravens again," Pippa murmured, glancing up at the carved wooden beams overhead. "They are everywhere in this place. The Pendletons must have been obsessed."

"And the acorn?" Alistair asked, already scanning the spines of the books for anything resembling one. "Or does the sword mean anything, do you think? There was a reference to Veritas and swords in the riddle pack with the Tarot Card, Veritas is truth?"

"I don't know," she said. "But I do know the Codex is real. It is bound in tan vellum, engraved with glyphs from a lost tribe, and neither the university nor Alfred Pendleton ever deciphered the underlying meaning of the symbols before the Codex was stolen in 1946."

Pippa moved swiftly now, fingers brushing over cracked bindings, her eyes searching for something that felt out of place; something old, but not obvious. Faded blue leather tomes caught her eye, several with gilded titles barely legible, but none bore the weight or feel of the Codex she imagined in her head. The threads of age seemed cornered in every book. It was as if time had left its mark on each of them, all those pages holding their own footprint of stories from the past: some read so often the spines were worn; others waiting patiently, untouched, full of potential. Lined and stacked in shelving holding them all together to form a universe of intrigue, memories and meaning.

Alistair took a more methodical approach, crouching low, scanning the bottom shelf for carvings, a tiny acorn detail, anything. "There must be something hidden," he muttered. "The missing acorn, it is a gap. A space. A clue in absence, not presence."

Pippa stood on tiptoe, reaching towards a high shelf where a slender wedge of gloomy light from the tall and night-darkened window cascaded down. She shone her torch, illuminating the area further, noticing the dust was thicker here. As she swept her torch light into the secluded corner, it settled on the spines of around five thick tomes.

She stood motionless, captivated. One of the books was conspicuously larger than the other. Its leather cover had a strange sheen, almost iridescent under the light; a rich lapis blue, devoid of markings on the spine except for a tiny oak tree, an acorn, and the silhouette of a raven. Something about it pulsed with a quiet gravity and expectation.

"Alistair," she whispered. "I think I found something."

Alistair moved sharply to stand next to Pippa, just as

excited and slightly nervous. Pippa reached for the book. It was heavy, its binding thick with dust. It wasn't ancient, but she thought it could be another clue. On the front was a gilded sword and the word 'Veritas'. Pippa felt Alistair's breath on her cheekbone. He was holding his emotion in check. Her heart pounded as she opened the book, and they realised simultaneously that within the folds of paper nestled inside was a cloth-wrapped bundle, secured with a black ribbon. A book within a book!

Alistair and Pippa exchanged a look, eyes wide, both now in tremors at what they were unearthing.

"Oh wow, this is it," Pippa whispered.

She placed the book – no, the box, into Alistair's hands, and carefully untied the ribbon. Her hands quietly trembling, she unwrapped the cloth, revealing the most beautiful artefact she had ever seen: aged tan vellum, etched with gold leaf and Mayan symbols, the wood pulp pages hand-inked with secrets lost to time. Alistair took a sharp breath, afraid that even the sound of exhaling might shatter the slightly magical feeling of discovery.

Suddenly, Oscar was hissing, and there was only one reason he would be doing that. The inspector was nearby, or someone else was coming. Alistair glanced at Pippa.

"I can hear movement upstairs, guys get a move on." Oscar whispered theatrically, a slight tremor in his voice.

Pippa and Alistair had no intention of being caught, especially now they had the Codex. Pippa's heart was pounding out of her chest and her inner voice screaming on a frantic loop: *fuck, fuck, FUCK!* The Codex, real, ancient, alive with meaning, cradled in her hands like a secret too sacred to exist.

Alistair did not waste a second. Taking it from Pippa's

shaking hands, he pulled out his phone, turned on the flash and began snapping photos of the Codex, working quickly but with care. His fingers flicked through the thick pages as gently as possible, wary of damaging the fragile item. The central spread glowed with gilded edges and vivid pigments, an intricate painting of Mayan symbols, rich with meaning he could not yet decipher.

He did not need to. He was certain that with time and research, the Codex would reveal what he already half-suspected: a truth buried deep, waiting to be uncovered.

Oscar hovered by the door, tense, listening for more footsteps. "We don't have much time," he hissed. "Someone's coming."

"What do we do now?" Alistair whispered.

"We can't put it back," Pippa said, her voice hushed but nervous as she retrieved the cloth and ribbon and wrapped the Codex back up. "We have to come clean. This belongs to the University. It is a discovery, Alistair, a real one, lost for years and now an opportunity to put it back where it belongs."

He nodded, heart thumping. "We haven't done anything wrong," he added, "except for being in the middle of a crime scene."

Oscar at this point gestured wildly with his hands for them to hurry up.

They slipped from the library like ghosts, Pippa clutching the Codex beneath her jumper, down the hallway towards the back stairs. Footsteps echoed above and there was the movement of someone coming down the main stairway.

"I'll distract whoever is coming, while you two get back to your rooms. It's not worth us all getting caught,"

Alistair volunteered.

Oscar gripped Alistair's shoulder, voice low and urgent, "Are you sure? What if you get arrested?"

"Go, quick, it will be fine, I have a hell of a headache so need some paracetamol and water from the kitchen anyway." Alistair nodded, the weight of what they had just done settling on his shoulders. "The brandy's finally catching up with me and the last twenty adrenaline-packed minutes have nearly finished me off."

Without waiting for a reply, Alistair rubbed his temple and hunched his shoulders, moving with the slow, groggy movements of someone nursing a vicious hangover. He skirted quietly around the corridor, looping towards the kitchen entrance. His steps echoed just enough to be heard.

From the stairwell, Detective Inspector Stevenson paused mid-step. He could hear footsteps. He frowned, instincts prickling, and altered his course, moving quickly down the stairs, towards the kitchen.

Someone was wandering the halls.

And they should not have been.

"Mr Fradley, what are you doing wandering about at this hour? You should be in your room." Dougie's voice cut through the quiet.

Alistair straightened, his posture stiff. His bloodshot eyes met the Inspector's without flinching. "I was getting a paracetamol. I have the worst headache, too much wine and brandy with dinner. I did not want to wake the whole house, so I crept downstairs."

Detective Stevenson fixed Alistair with a firm look. "You need to return to your room immediately. There has been a murder, and no-one should be wandering about the house. I will speak with you further about this in the morning."

"On my way, Detective." Alistair moved on.

Up the back staircase, Pippa and Oscar silently retreated. Their footsteps were light, barely audible on the carpeted steps. Pippa slipped into her room, closed the door softly behind her, and sat on the bed with the Codex clutched in her hands. Her heart was still thumping loudly in her ears. She wondered how she could explain that it had been found; how she could reveal it to the authorities without stirring more chaos. It was something to deal with after the murder is solved. Maybe. For now, she needed to sleep. If sleep was even possible.

Oscar, by contrast, collapsed straight into bed, eyes shut before his head fully hit the pillow. *What the hell am I doing in this drama?* he thought but within moments he was drifting into uneasy dreams.

CHAPTER 19

The Next Morning

Vivienne followed Gina into the kitchen. She needed to be near her rational friend. Gina already had bacon in the Aga, bread on the table, ready for breakfast.

"What are we to do?! This is going from bad to worse; everyone stuck here and a dead body in the library … a dead Jeremy!"

Gina started to cut up the loaf of bread. Vivienne half-heartedly began to gather crockery and cutlery.

"The Chesters seemed such an unassuming pair, hardly the type to bump somebody off. They must have had something against him. Mind you, most people who've met him have something against Jeremy!" Vivienne mused.

"Well, sexual predators do tend to attract intense dislike," Gina replied mildly.

Vivienne knew that Gina was a good judge of character and had obviously seen right through Jeremy. She only wished she had done the same all those years before.

"Thank God we have the Aga," Gina continued. "With the power still off, it would have been a nightmare to feed this lot, and soon they'll be moaning like hell there's no hot water. Can you help me carry these to the dining room, Viv?"

DI Stevenson was woken up by a sharp dig in the ribs, "Wake up, lazy bones."

Ellie stood over him, fully dressed and eager to get going. She had got up early and showered. Gina had provided a toothbrush and paste, and apart from having to wear the same clothes, Ellie felt refreshed, her still-damp hair pulled into a band behind her head.

The aroma of coffee and bacon drifted up from the kitchen, and it spurred Dougie into movement. He swung the warm blankets off and sat up. He looked up at his sergeant, who was still stood waiting for him.

"I'm off to get breakfast," Ellie replied. "Why don't you go and use the shower in my room? You need it, boss." Before Dougie could reply, Ellie was off, smirking to herself, imagining his reaction when he realised there was no hot water.

When a somewhat chilly, but considerably more awake Dougie returned to his makeshift bedroom, Gina was there, holding a tray with a steaming pot of tea and a bacon sandwich. His stomach growled.

"Thought you might appreciate this, not sure you can have slept much there," Gina nodded to the couch.

"I've slept in worse places," he replied, taking the tray from her gratefully.

"Where are you from, Gina? There's a Northern twang there if I'm not mistaken?"

Gina laughed softly, "Still? I thought it was all gone. I was brought up in a little village in Lancashire – it feels like a hundred years ago now. You, where are you from?"

"Cambridgeshire born and bred; the Fens, I've got webbed feet! What I'd really like is mountains, and sea. Maybe we all want what we can't have…" His sentence trailed off.

After breakfast, Dougie and Ellie wandered onto the terrace. The weather was finally calmer, although there was still a fresh breeze. They both felt like they needed the fresh air; the atmosphere in the house was oppressive.

"What now sir?" Ellie had tucked her shirt in roughly and tried but failed to align the seams of her trousers.

Dougie smiled as he looked at her crumpled appearance. Ellie was pretty, despite looking just then as though she had been dragged through a hedge backwards.

"I have just spoken to the desk sergeant, still zero chance of backup. It's chaos out there, trees down, abandoned cars, flooding. Let's go back into the library and take a look at that body first."

DI Stevenson, wearing regulation rubber gloves, dipped under the crime scene tape, opened the library door, and stood on the threshold. Ellie followed him in, her notebook already in hand. Once in the library they closed the door and turned to face the corpse. The smell of congealed blood filled their nostrils.

Early morning light gave Dougie a better view of the room than he had had the night before and, straightening his tie, he stepped forward, his brogues soundless. He swept his eyes across the room. The victim lay slumped in the leather armchair. No sign of a struggle, no overturned furniture. Just the quiet hush of a room that held something else: death. Stevenson approached the body, kneeling carefully beside the armchair. His eyes scanned the victim, the glass, the faint traces of something spilled on the rug. Whisky, he guessed. Further stains of blood, and a lot of it, marked where the corpse's head rested. Dougie examined the body again, this time with gloves. He lifted the head away from the back of the chair. Dried blood and brains had stuck to the leather, and it took effort. "The back of his head is completely caved in," he told Ellie, recoiling slightly at the sight; it didn't get any easier, being this close to death. "Have you got your phone handy? Take photos of this, will you?"

While Dougie indicated what he needed to record, including the dislodged fender with its small and ugly decoration of hair and blood, Ellie took the shots. "Whoever did this was not messing about. Look around for any sign of a murder weapon, would you?"

Stevenson stood and moved towards the desk, its surface disturbingly neat, the leather inlay faded except for a single clearly defined spot where a roughly oval shape stood out in sharp contrast to the rest, the green leather around faded by years of sunlight. What had stood there all that time but was no longer there? The murder weapon, perhaps?

"Have you checked for any sign of forced entry?"

"None," Ellie said. "Windows are all locked from the inside."

As Ellie spoke, Dougie glanced involuntarily towards the window on the far side of the desk. He saw a smear on the central pane, just above eye level, and walked over to have a closer look; it was definitely blood and more than a squashed fly could account for. He asked Ellie to photograph it.

Stevenson crossed the room to the bookcases, running his fingers along the leatherbound spines. "See that?"

A book was slightly out of line, pulled just half an inch further than the others. Ellie stepped forward and gently pulled it free. It was box-like, with an untied ribbon. The box was empty.

"A hiding place, and someone knew it was there," Stevenson said.

Ellie nodded, scribbling quickly. "Could be what they were after."

"Bag that, Ellie, It might be significant and it might have fingerprints."

"What do you make of the Chesters' confessions?" he asked as they continued to search for anything which might be significant. "I can't pin down the time of their supposed assault, but events suggest Pendleton survived it to make the phone call." He pointed to the bloody smear on the window. "It's possible he walked over there after the assault. Forensics will confirm. Maybe, he lost consciousness after the call?"

"Hm, that wound on his forehead looks superficial. The wound to the back of his head bled like hell, so he must have been alive when he received that blow. Do you think the Chesters went back and finished him off? They were very keen to confess."

"They have got a damn good motive though. Unrecognised, illegitimate son and he admits he saw red. I don't buy her story, she was just protecting him. Besides, there's nothing of her; not sure she could have floored the victim, even at his age. The inheritance claim seems spurious to me, just like Jeremy's own." Dougie continued, "Right, enough speculation, we need facts. You get witness statements from the rest of them and remember they are all suspects, not just the posh ones!"

Ellie smiled wryly as he reminded her of her one professional bias.

"What are you going to do, sir?"

"I think it's time I had a look at the victim's room."

The old house groaned softly from the wind outside, its aged bones whispering stories to those willing to listen. They stepped into the shadowed hallway of Ravenshade Manor and Ellie shivered.

CHAPTER 20

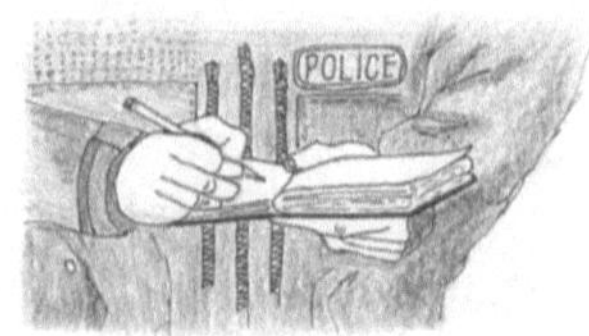

DS Ford pulled off her gloves and put them into a plastic bag, stuffing it temporarily into her trouser pocket. She and her boss agreed: the story the Chesters had told them did not fit with the injuries they had seen. The fatal blow was the injury to the back of the skull and unless they had gone back to finish off the victim, the couple would only be open to a charge of GBH at worst. Ellie was ready to take statements from all the suspects, knowing that she would have to speak to Madeline and Harrison again. She heaved a sigh as she crossed the entrance hall floor to the staircase. It was bad enough investigating a murder without having to weed out folk almost desperate to be accused.

Ellie headed straight for Madeline's room, repeating her boss's words to herself. "Be polite. Be curious. Be open minded." Sadly, she promptly forgot these principles as, filled with frustration, she walked in to see Madeline jump up from the unmade bed, looking dishevelled, scared, and like she had not slept a wink.

"I don't know what I'm supposed to do. Will you be taking me to prison now?"

Ellie tutted her annoyance, her tone more clipped than she intended, "Come with me to the drawing room, please. We need to have a chat. No need for drama. Get dressed, I'll wait outside."

They sat in the same positions they had the previous night, this time illuminated by the bright morning light flooding the room from the floor-to-ceiling windows.

"I need you to repeat your understanding, or memory, about what happened in the library last night." Madeline again told her story and Ellie patiently took notes. There was nothing new and Madeline stuck doggedly to her story that she, not her husband, had been responsible. When she had finished, Ellie suggested that she return upstairs to her room and rest.

Ellie sighed. She was sure the woman was not telling the truth. A head appeared round the door. It was Gina Meredith.

"I thought you might be ready for this?" she smiled, coming into the room, bearing a tray with tea and cake.

Ellie decided to seize the opportunity. "Do you have a few minutes to spare, Ms Meredith… Gina? I need to take a statement from you and now seems as good a time as any."

"Of course," Gina replied, taking the seat Madeline had just vacated.

Pouring the tea, Ellie asked, "How well did you know Jeremy Pendleton?"

"I had a few conversations with him, regarding his involvement in this week's retreat, and we exchanged emails about his accommodation, timings, his fee. You know, practicalities like that."

"You'd never met him before then?"

"Not before he arrived yesterday, although I have read all his books. Makes you think though, doesn't it?"

"What does?" said Ellie

"Well, you know. That perhaps there is such a thing as natural justice; from talking to the others, he seems to have been a nasty piece of work."

Ellie didn't want to go down this route. Facts, she needed facts. "How long have you worked here?"

"Over twenty years now. Vivienne... Ms Henderson... and I met when she came to a house party at an estate where I worked previously. We hit it off immediately and she asked me to come and help her run this place."

"And you live here?" Ellie asked, making a note.

"Yeah! Perk of the job. I have an office-cum-sitting room downstairs and a bedroom upstairs, overlooking the lake. Vivienne and I mostly spend time together in the kitchen though, it's the warmest room in the house."

"So, you and Ms Henderson greeted everyone as they arrived yesterday. Can you be more specific regarding times of arrival? And anything else you noticed?" Ellie said.

"Jeremy arrived first, about two o'clock. I showed him up to his room. Oscar Martin-Bramston also arrived early, at around 2.30pm. He was hoping for a tour of the place, but Vivienne didn't have time to take him, and the weather wasn't great to be outside. Mali Pritchard next, almost on the dot of 3pm. She looked weary, she had had a long drive from Wales somewhere, I believe. Expensive clothes and luggage. Mr and Mrs Chester arrived soon after Mali; odd pair, I thought. His father was the travel writer, Grayson Chester." Gina looked at Ellie expectantly.

Ellie shrugged. "I am not much of a reader, to be honest."

"Alistair Fradley was next. He came by taxi. He seemed anxious when he arrived; keyed up, you know. He was smoking on the porch when I went to open the door. He is an old friend of Vivienne's, same hippie circuit back in the day. Pippa Whitcombe was the last to arrive; typical, she only came from town, and she rolled up just as everything was starting. Students, eh?"

"Can you tell me about dinner? Where was everyone sitting?"

"I did a seating plan." Gina fished a piece of paper out of her pocket and held it out to Ellie. "After dinner, I served coffee and drinks in the drawing room, but Vivienne and Alistair went outside for a smoke; thick as thieves, those two." Gina smiled indulgently. "Jeremy excused himself and said he was going to the library to prepare for the session he was to run. Come to think of it, I don't think Mali stayed long in the drawing room, she left just after Jeremy and didn't rejoin the rest of us until later, said she was going to bed, but she must have changed her mind, as she came back later - she was certainly in the drawing room when the power went off."

One by one, Ellie took statements from the rest of the guests. She needed a break but had one more interview to conduct. Pippa Whitcombe's. Ellie had thought that her boss should take Pippa's statement, as she was the one who found the body, but then thought better of it. He had trusted her to take statements from everyone so, gritting her teeth, she went in search of the young woman.

Once again, DS Ford sat in the drawing room, opposite

a suspected killer. "Thank you for joining me here, Pippa. May I call you Pippa?"

"Yes, of course."

"I know you've had a terrible shock, and talking about it is undoubtedly the last thing you want to do. But I am sure you want to help us find out who caused the death of Mr Pendleton. To do that I need to ask you a few questions." Ellie smiled reassuringly to put Pippa at ease. "Did you know Jeremy Pendleton, Pippa?"

"No. I had never met him before. I came here to see him, though. He was the reason I joined this retreat. I had tracked a trail of obscure clues, scattered across old correspondences and records, all pointing to Ravenshade Manor, and to him. The missing Mayan Codex manuscript, stolen from the university library in 1946. The whole thing reeks of secrecy. Mr Pendleton was meant to be the key to unlocking what really happened."

"And now, he is dead."

"Yes."

"So let me get this straight. You are here because of a lost and valuable manuscript, is that correct?"

"That is right, Detective. The Mayan Codex is not just valuable, it is priceless. A singular artifact, centuries old, and brimming with knowledge we barely understand. There is also a rumour that it has a treasure map on it. It vanished without a trace in 1946, right out of the university's archives, and no-one has ever answered for it. Until recently, I had nothing but dead ends, until Jeremy's name surfaced. He was the son of the librarian in charge at the time. He held a piece of the puzzle. That is why I came here, to Ravenshade. To speak with him. I am the editor of the *Gilded Quill*, and I am writing an article for the university, hence my interest. Unfortunately, someone got to him first."

"What time did you arrive here?"

"About 6.30. I was running late; the drive from town was a nightmare. The storm had already started by the time I left Cambridge. The roads were waterlogged. At one point I was not sure I would make it, but I am quite determined. When I finally reached the manor, the place looked almost swallowed by the storm. I made my own way into the hallway, then I heard voices coming from the drawing room. I knew I was late and from the sound of it the gathering had already started."

God, she is dramatic, thought Ellie, *a head full of mystery and intrigue.*

"What time did you leave the dinner table? Did anyone observe you leave, or were you with anyone?"

"It was around nine o'clock. Dessert had just been cleared away and I went with the others to the drawing room for coffee and chatted with Oscar. He can confirm that, if needed. But truthfully, my mind was not on coffee. I needed to get into the library. I had reason to believe the Codex, or at least a clue to its whereabouts, might be hidden somewhere in that room."

"And later, what time did you leave the drawing room to go into the library, Pippa?"

"It must have been around 10:20pm, or thereabouts. The clock had already struck 10:15. The storm was louder, rattling the windows, creaking through the manor. I was slightly spooked, to be honest. Almost as soon as I had turned the lights on in the library, the power went off. I used the light on my phone to guide me. The embers of a fire still smouldered in the hearth, casting a faint light. I felt a presence and turned, and that is when I saw the body, in the armchair, slumped and completely still. I froze. 'Hello,' I said. It was quite surreal. I repeated myself but no response. I moved closer and then I realised he was dead."

CHAPTER 21

The silence of the victim's bedroom pressed against DI Stevenson like a held breath. The previous night's storm had abated, leaving a soaked, windblown landscape. Morning light filtered through the tall windows, illuminating a room preserved in tasteful disarray, with the faintest hint of lavender in the air. The murder had been brutal. Pendleton's skull cracked open with a heavy object which was, without doubt, the cause of death.

For this reason, although Harrison and Madeline Chester had owned up to the crime, and had a motive, if somewhat tenuous, the evidence told the detective otherwise. The fall onto the fireplace did not seem enough to be fatal. What had sat so heavily as to leave its imprint on the leather-topped desk in the library? Its absence whispered violence in DI Stevenson's ear as persistently as the victim's bloodied head screamed murder.

The detective trusted the personal spaces. Bedrooms spoke when mouths refused. He stepped inside, eyes scanning for anything out of place. A wardrobe half-open revealed two neatly hung suits and two pairs of perfectly polished shoes. A chest of drawers, the top cluttered with loose papers, pens, and several notebooks with no titles. Even more notebooks were in a holdall on the floor. Inside a bedroom side table he found another book labelled, 'Diary 2025'. Inside it, Dougie found an entry dated for the following week. An appointment with Pendleton's solicitor. He picked up his mobile and made a quick call.

A half-empty bottle of Highland Park whisky was on the bedside table. Stevenson looked at it for almost a minute, tempted. He groaned. What evil demon had ensured he would come face to face with his ambrosia and, yes, this wrecker of lives, at such a solitary point in a murder investigation? He needed courage and wisdom and here they lay – in a bottle of golden liquid that called to him like a siren. Dougie turned away and mentally tied himself to the mast of his faltering ship. It was four years since his marriage had ended and two since a drop of alcohol had passed his lips. He was a recovering alcoholic, he reminded himself, and this was evidence that needed preserving. He slipped on a pair of regulation gloves and popped the bottle into an evidence bag. Still with gloved hands, he gathered together the papers from the chest of drawers. Glancing through them, he realised they were a typed draft of the man's autobiography.

Stevenson yawned loudly. The night before had been taxing and he had tossed and turned on the couch, dreaming of whispers and footsteps through the corridors of an old house. Stevenson sat on the bed. He opened one of the nondescript notebooks carefully. The book's pages were dated irregularly, like diary entries, but read like a memoir. He flipped through the first few pages, absorbing fragments.

We were gods then or thought ourselves so. In the summers of '79 and '80, we drank port in Cambridge gardens and lied to one another about the future. Alistair, and Vivienne... always Vivienne.

October 10th, 1980. Wine and nibbles with the provost and newbies this evening. Usual bores. Main topic of conversation was the Tory party conference. But I did spot a gorgeous young woman hovering in the shadows. Fradley's little sister, I think. Perhaps this lady at least will be for turning. Watch this space.

May 1st, 1981. Fradley was hysterical in my rooms this morning. Accused me of betraying him and his sister. Seems she has 'confessed' to him the reason for her ongoing depression. Such melodrama. Did I know she was only 18? Of course, I bloody did. Apparently, I broke her heart. He's threatening to go to the master. Not if I get him sent down first.

Stevenson contemplated this information. 1980... 45 years ago. Flaming hell. Bitter lovers, not to mention their big brothers, do not always forgive, and some never forget. Someone coming back to settle an old score would fit. But then, why now? Why kill him after decades? A sibling bent on revenge, letting it fester all these years? Or maybe the affair was not entirely consensual – rape was a powerful motive for murder.

Stevenson brushed away a memory of his own breach of trust four years ago, losing him the love of his life. He had spent years building his reputation as a dedicated Detective Inspector, trusted and respected by his colleagues. But he had made a choice and strayed, not considering how it would touch the life he shared with the woman he adored. A moment of madness, which had cost him dearly. The woman who had stood by him through long nights, missed dinners and the weight of the job. When the truth surfaced it wasn't anger in her eyes that broke him, but the quiet devastation. He watched her walk away, realising too late that he had not only lost her trust, but the future of which they had dreamed. He shook his head, determinedly turning his attention back to the investigation.

He quickly read on and learned that the murder victim also had a relationship with Vivienne Henderson, Ravenshade's owner and, to Stevenson surprise, he found that they were, in fact, cousins.

July 8th, 1979. Never thought I could have an enjoyable time here at Ravenshade, or that cousins could be so affectionate. I almost forgive Viv for inheriting this pile, given the fun we had today. My God! I am all for a Bohemian lifestyle if you can pick up the tricks she has learned.

The diary went on to present Viviene as manipulative and somewhat ruthless and made it clear that he believed himself to be the rightful owner of Ravenshade Manor. By the side of this entry, he had added a recent note, pencilled in the margin.

October 27ʰ, 2025. Just had a shock.

Viv didn't offer a very warm welcome. Standing in the entrance of what should have been my home, looking like a ship in full sail and ready to do battle. Those dresses she wears- they do nothing for her now everything's heading south. Told me the other writer Freddie Hughes (female apparently) is not coming because of the weather. Had the cheek to tell me she was the lead speaker. I could leave now but I'm curious to see this place again. Maybe the old man left that Codex here after all? It is bucketing down here, hope the roof doesn't leak.

Dougie set aside the notebook and searched among the papers for a reference he had spotted moments before – here it was in another book:

That blasted Codex dominated my father's life. He never admitted stealing it, of course, but the guilt clung to him like tobacco smoke. It cursed him, I think. And probably me too. His scholarship got in the way of him seeing what was happening to me at the hands of his friends.

Fradley knew about the Codex. He hinted at it, said knowledge like that should be shared, not hoarded. He was always looking to damage me. We had some terrible rows.

Engrossed now, Stevenson kicked off his shoes, the book still in his hands. He rubbed his eyes and without thinking moved fully onto the bed. He lay back, propping himself up against the headboard. The room exhaled around him, the silence deepening as he thought about a stolen artifact and how a secret buried in the past might affect his investigation. Wondering briefly how Ellie was getting on, he lifted the notebook and read on.

August 10th, 1985. It's 11.00pm and I am spent. Mr and Mrs M were at market today and left me with their delectable daughter. I could almost sense the local lads circling. Decided to do her a favour. Found her in the barn lugging out a hay bale. She was sweaty with the effort and looked pleased to see me, asked me for help. Well, how could I refuse, I helped her didn't I? We had a joke about Madonna (she never stops singing that awful song "In the groove") and I told her what Madonna really means. It is not a cheap label for a pop singer. By this point I seemed to have removed her T shirt and shorts. Let us say she was never going to be in the running for a Madonna figure. She cried afterwards and I did the usual comforting stuff. There, there, it is all right, etc. I was her first. She will get over it, let those gagging local lads in now.

Stevenson shook his head, appalled, and turned another page. A floorboard creaked faintly in the hallway beyond the bedroom door. Stevenson did not move. He closed the book and placed it on the nightstand, then sat up, suddenly alert. He was now aware of motives that spanned generations. He needed to speak to the Chesters again. Something was off, but Stevenson didn't know what. There were pages missing from a couple of the diaries – 2012 and also this year; they had obviously been recently and hurriedly torn out. The weight of the memoir still in his thoughts, he bent down to retrieve his shoes, and saw, poking out from under the bedspread, a mobile phone. He pulled out an evidence bag from his pocket and slipped the phone inside. This wasn't just a murder anymore. It was an unravelling of secrets and lies spanning generations.

The grandfather clock in the hall below struck 11.30 and the bedroom door opened suddenly, startling him out of his musings. Ellie appeared at the door.

"Been having a nap, sir?" she asked, grinning.

Ellie noticed the half empty bottle of Highland Park whisky, already bagged, on the bedside table, and realised Jeremy must have been four sheets to the wind at the time of his death… unless?

Dougie followed her gaze. "No, Ellie, I haven't been helping myself."

"Whatever, you look pretty comfy there though, sir. Want to hear what I've learnt? Budge up." Dougie shifted his weight and Ellie sat on the edge of the bed beside him.

"I've re-interviewed the Chesters, who are sticking to their stories, and I've interviewed everyone else. I think we can discount Pippa Whitcombe; she's got no motive, in fact she needed him alive. She was on about a Codex, though."

"A Mayan Codex is mentioned in one of these books I've been reading. It looks as though the victim was getting ready to write a 'warts and all' memoir," Dougie told her.

Ellie could not contain her frustration at yet another mention of the Codex. "Come on sir, we haven't all been to fancy universities. What the hell is a Codex?" she asked, frowning.

"It's a very valuable folding book from a medieval South American civilisation that, according to Pendleton's diary, his father might have stolen and hidden here. We need to find out if it is here, its presence could be a motive. Carry on. What else?"

"Mali Pritchard was seen going upstairs after dinner, by Gina Meredith. Worryingly, she's into herbs and homemade lotions which she carries around with her.

Apparently for sensitive skin and she said she takes some homemade remedy to help her sleep. Found an article about it, appears the sleeping draught has been used since medieval times. She said, 'One shot and you're chilled, two shots and'…"

Ellie let that hang for a moment before continuing, "She says she's here to learn about novel-writing but then started to talk about her grandparents' relationship with the dead man's father. Honestly, I swear most of these people are linked in some way. Plus, she is convinced that the victim might have been able to tell her a few things about her brother's death. It seems that Jeremy Pendleton was the last person to see Owain Pritchard alive. He was only fifteen when he died. Sad… Said she was here to confront him," Ellie consulted her notes – "before quickly changing 'confront' to 'speak with'. She said she had the impression that most of the other guests knew him to different degrees. Definitely worth further questioning, sir."

Dougie made a mental note. Mali had the opportunity then to go into the victim's room. Was she the one who had ripped pages out of the notebook? Was the victim drugged to make killing him easy?

"OK. Vivienne Henderson has known Pendleton for years. She must have known him before he started writing. They spent time together at the far end of the hippy era. She had an affair with him, and she reckons he was an arrogant prick. She is short of money and finding it difficult to keep this place going. She says she went outside with Alistair after dinner, but they are each other's alibis for that. Supposedly had a fag, and then went their separate ways, him back to the house and her to her camper van. What sort of stately homeowner chooses to live in a manky camper van in the grounds? Ms Henderson got wet in the storm and went to the kitchen to dry off and is certain of the time because that clock in the hall chimed the hour. She says she saw the Chesters reach the top of the stairs as she headed back to the drawing room. Again, no alibi, and she didn't reappear in the drawing room until just before the lights went out at 10:20. If she did see the Chesters on the stairs, that would fit with them at least having been downstairs but not in the drawing room when Pendleton was initially attacked. It's a narrow window of opportunity, sir - his call came into Parkside a few minutes later."

"I can add to the information about Vivienne Henderson," Dougie said, interrupting Ellie's flow. "Pendleton had an appointment booked in his diary to see his solicitor next week. I've spoken to him, a chap called Toth. He says Pendleton was going to change his will. Henderson had been his sole beneficiary, but he had recently had a crisis of conscience and wanted to 'make amends' to his old university. He was going to leave everything to them. Toth told me Pendleton had frequent spiritual crises, and this was the latest of them. 'Fits of pique more like,' Toth said. He implied Pendleton was a sad character who was becoming more and more obsessed over the whereabouts of the Codex, which he wanted to return to its rightful owner, the university library. As Toth said, 'How could he bequeath an object that legally didn't belong to him, not to mention the fact that it hasn't been seen for nearly 80 years?' All tied up with this tell-all book he planned to write, so Toth thinks."

"Why was Henderson in his will? Do you think she knew about it, sir? It gives her one hell of a motive, if she still thought she stood to benefit from his death."

Dougie gestured at the notebooks around him. "It seems she was his cousin and possibly his only surviving relative. We need to keep her in mind, but give me a summary of the other statements."

"Right, Oscar Martin-double barrel-Bramston. He claims to have been drawn to the writers' retreat by the other author, Freddie Hughes. Anyway, he says he is thinking of writing a book. States he knew the victim thirty years ago but has never seen him since. Pretty clear he thinks Pendleton was a nasty piece of work. Either he knew him better than he is letting on, or whatever happened between them all those years ago left a nasty taste. Also, he is here to check out a venue for his next art exhibition. A decent cover story if one is needed, don't you think, sir? He left the drawing room when the power went off. He went with Gina Meredith to find candles in the kitchen. Confirmed by the others. Ms Meredith, Gina. She's OK, I like her." Dougie raised his eyebrows and Ellie quickly continued. "She seems level-headed, worked her way up. She is Vivienne's workhorse and organised the writers' retreat."

"Get to the point, please Ellie. Facts." Dougie said patiently.

Ellie selected and chewed the nearest strand of hair, "Gina seems to have noticed all the comings and goings. She was in and out all evening, making sure the guests were all fed, watered and comfortable. She had never met Pendleton before yesterday. She has read his books though. She seems to get on well with her boss, although

I think some of these posh clients get up her nose a bit – I know how she feels. She gave me a bit of a run down on all the suspects."

"Ellie, you are letting your class warrior take charge. Don't forget Gina's a suspect too."

"Yes sir, you're right. So, she gave me the order of arrival and a sketch plan of the seating at dinner. She noticed friction between Pendleton and Fradley, tension between the victim and Mrs Chester, understandable as we now know, she described Henderson and Fradley as thick as thieves."

"Please try to stick to facts, Ellie." Dougie stood for a moment and stretched his legs. His stomach rumbled. He moved to sit in an upright chair placed next to the wardrobe and glanced at his watch.

"Going back to Alistair Fradley, sir. I did not like him."

Dougie audibly sighed. "Ellie?"

"Well, he was 'Can I call you Ellie?' this and 'Please call me Alistair,' that. I thought he was shifty, could have been nerves I suppose. He is here to meet other writers. He thinks he bumped into Pendleton on the way back from having a fag with Vivienne, and had a few words with him, but he was vague and looked uncomfortable when I pressed him. Actually, everyone still in the drawing room – Martin-Bramston, Henderson, Pritchard, the Chesters, Whitcombe and Meredith – all heard raised voices coming from the hall and Alistair looked agitated when he rejoined them."

Dougie thought back to what he had read in Pendleton's notebooks about Fradley and his sister. Perhaps Fradley did have unfinished business with the victim.

Ellie's phone rang, making them both jump. Dougie watched her take the call, combining intent listening with brief questions and comments. She was a good police officer, he thought, she just needed to shed that chip on her shoulder.

"That was Parkside, sir. Martin-Bramston was arrested in 1993 during a protest to drop the age of consent for gay men. Alistair Fradley and Vivienne Henderson have old convictions for possession of dope, no surprise there. Nothing on the others. The desk sergeant's had a flash of inspiration. He telephoned Pendleton's old college and spoke to the Master. He said Pendleton lectured there until 2000. There were rumours of 'ungentlemanly behaviour', but he was never openly accused. Some of his students adored him but others would not be left alone with him. Eventually he left by mutual agreement. Honestly, sir, what a creep, and they just swept it under the carpet."

"That creep, as you call him, is dead and cold downstairs. Murdered. Whatever he did, he's more than paid for it." He gave his Sargeant a hard stare and there was a long pause, before Inspector Stevenson spoke again,

"Now, I think we are close, Ellie." He trailed off, lost in thought. "Pretty much everyone seems to have a motive, but we can see who had opportunity. Yes, I think it's pretty clear now."

Ellie just gazed at her boss, none the wiser.

A light knock on the door had them both standing. Gina Meredith opened the door and stood looking at them. "Just letting you know, the power is back on, and lunch is ready."

"Thank God," Dougie and Ellie said simultaneously.

CHAPTER 22

The dining room fell silent as Detective Inspector Stevenson, Detective Sergeant Ford, and Harrison and Madeline Chester walked inside. Everyone stopped eating, suddenly losing their appetite.

Harrison stepped forward. "We are in the clear," he said loudly. "We didn't kill Jeremy, and that means one of you is the murderer." Madeline held on to her husband's arm.

The police officers moved to the end of the table, facing them all, their presence commanding attention. Eight anxious faces turned towards them. A man was dead, and the list of people who might have wanted him gone seemed endless. It was Stevenson's task to cut through the half-truths and silence until the truth surfaced. The DI's gaze swept the room before he spoke.

"Yes, I can confirm that Mr and Mrs Chester didn't kill Mr Pendleton. One of you did."

Calm but authoritative, Stevenson began to explain how every clue had led them to this moment: the lies; the hidden motives; the small slip that finally betrayed the killer.

"Oscar Martin-Bramston. You had an intimate relationship with the victim in 1993. Pendleton rejected you and you came here to Ravenshade for one purpose only. To take revenge?" Stevenson stared at him.

"No Inspector, you've got it wrong. Ok yes, we had a relationship , and it ended badly, but I could never hurt him. I intend to hold my next art exhibition here at Ravenshade, and I came primarily to discuss that with Ms Henderson."

"Your history with the victim gave you a motive, but fortunately for you, you have an alibi. I have witness statements confirming you didn't leave the drawing room for the whole evening, except to fetch candles with Gina after the power went off."

"Mr Fradley, you too were friends with the victim many years ago." DI Stevenson studied Alistair carefully. The twitch of a leg he couldn't keep still.

Alistair pushed his chair back and crossed his legs. "Yes. Jeremy, Vivienne and I used to hang around together, but like you've pointed out, that was a long time ago."

"You left the drawing room with Ms Henderson and went outside for a cigarette. Strange, as there was a storm raging outside. Then Ms Henderson left you to go to her camper van and you came back inside. Neither of you have an alibi for that time. Also, there was some animosity between you and the victim, wasn't there? An argument was overheard just before the murder. What was that about?"

"Vivienne and I sheltered in the Hunt Room to have a smoke, and it wasn't an argument I had with Pendleton exactly. I never liked the way he treated Vivienne. He was a pompous git, and I told him so. He was a plagiarist too, Inspector. Did you know that? Stole other writers' ideas and work, for his own use. And was successful at it. And what he did to my sister was… was… unforgiveable."

"Motive, Mr Fradley. But I'll leave it there for the moment."

Alistair's jaw tightened. A pulse flickered at his temple.

Stevenson turned his attention to Miss Whitcombe. This morning, she wore baggy oversized jeans and a white shirt with a huge, embroidered pocket, so out of place with the other guests. She had tied her hair back into a long ponytail. Her fresh face, devoid of makeup, gave her the appearance of being much younger than she was. "Miss Whitcombe."

"Yes, Inspector?"

"You found the body. Nobody knows exactly how long you were in the library before you screamed. You had opportunity. I understand from your witness statement to my sergeant that you joined the writers' retreat for the purpose of speaking to Mr Pendleton, regarding his father's time at Cambridge University, and his role in the disappearance of a Mayan Codex. Which sounds fascinating," Stevenson said cynically.

"I didn't kill him, Inspector."

"No, I don't think you did, Pippa."

DI Stevenson's eyes swept over the table. The tension was palpable. The people sitting around the table avoided eye contact with the Inspector, and with one another.

"Sergeant Ford. Please remind me of the details of Miss Pritchard's statement."

"Yes sir. Miss Pritchard says she is here because she wants to write a book about the natural herbs and grasses for use in medicine." Ellie glanced at Mali then continued, "Her grandparents knew Mr Pendleton's father, Alfred, and supported him when he was accused of stealing the Mayan manuscript. Her father also knew the victim. Miss Pritchard said she knew of his reputation as a writer and a man. He attended a school creative writing course while her brother was there, and her brother lost his life whilst on the course. She wanted to speak to Mr Pendleton about that but never got the chance. She thought he might remember something her brother had said, or something that had led to his death."

Mali sat up straight. She radiated sadness and unease. Stevenson pondered the implications, letting the silence stretch a moment until she broke it.

"You can't possibly think I had anything to do with this?"

"Carry on Ellie," Stevenson said.

"Miss Pritchard also stated that she didn't stay too long in the drawing room after dinner, but went upstairs to check she had something to help her sleep; a home-remedy. She came back downstairs to the drawing room about twenty minutes later; seems like a long time to check for a sleeping pill?"

"Did you go into Mr Pendleton's bedroom while you were upstairs?" Stevenson asked Mali.

"No, why would I?" Mali answered, blinking.

"I found pages missing from one of Mr Pendleton's notebooks. If I were to check the corresponding dates, would they coincide with the time your brother attended the writing course and met the victim?"

Mali looked defeated. "Yes," she whispered.

"So, you ripped out the pages. Why? Was it because they held information about your brother?"

"Yes. But I didn't kill him."

"I need those pages returned to my sergeant immediately, Miss Pritchard. They are part of an ongoing investigation. Think yourself lucky if I don't proceed to arrest you for perverting the course of justice. Fortunately, you too have an alibi."

Mali slumped in her chair, wiping tears from her eyes.

"Now before we move on, is there anything any of you want to add to your statement?" Stevenson asked. No-one replied. Vivienne felt DS Ford's eyes on her like an eagle's focused on its prey. She felt that Ellie could read her mind and in the process of trying hard to still her thoughts she became increasingly agitated. The room suddenly felt oppressive.

"Ok then. Ms Henderson. We've established that your guests, Oscar, Pippa, and Mali have alibis for the evening of the murder. You and Mr Fradley are each other's alibi until you separated..." Dougie let the sentence hang. "Yes. I went to my camper van to check it was alright, with the stormy conditions you know, it's in woodland over there." Vivienne waved, indicating somewhere on her right. "I was saturated when I got back to the house and ran to the kitchen to dry off."

"What time was this?"

"Like I told your sergeant, Inspector. I know exactly the time. It was ten o'clock on the dot. The grandfather clock was chiming as I made my way from the kitchen, where I had been drying off."

"Was Mr Pendleton in the drawing room when you entered?"

"No, I don't think he was." Her face frowned in concentration. "Oh! that's right, Alistair told me Jeremy had gone into the library to prepare for the next day."

"Did you go into the library, Ms Henderson, and murder Mr Pendleton, before joining the others in the drawing room?"

"No, no, no. Oh dear God, no, it wasn't me."

With furious indignation, Alistair jumped to his feet. "Detective Inspector, I implore you, please stop. What on earth has Vivienne to gain by killing her cousin?"

"Good point, Mr. Fradley. What does she gain now that her cousin in dead? Ms Meredith. May I call you Gina?" He turned his implacable gaze upon the woman, whose face was unreadable.

"Yes Inspector, of course."

"You have looked after all of us through this very traumatic time. And for that I am grateful. As you know, it is my job to solve crime and bring the guilty to justice. Earlier I asked if there was anything anyone wanted to add to their statement. I wasn't just asking the guests, Ms Meredith… Gina. I was asking you too."

"I don't have anything to add. Except to say you're barking up the wrong tree if you think Vivienne had anything to do with it. She wouldn't harm a fly."

"When I searched the victim's room. I came across a draft of a memoir Mr Pendleton was in the process of compiling. Also, I don't know if you all know this, but Mr Pendleton wrote everything down in notebooks, from as early as 1979, would you believe." Stevenson glanced at the group, all still sitting at the dining table, watching him. "It made for interesting reading. In August 1985, he stayed on a farm in the Ribble Valley with a Mr and Mrs M, in the north of England. He spent time with their daughter. You're from the Ribble Valley aren't you, Gina?

Would you know of a Mr and Mrs M who owned a farm there?"

Gina's face was impassive whilst the detective inspector spoke, her eyes fixed on a point above his head. The index finger of her left hand had worked at a little hole in the denim of her jeans. As he finished speaking, Gina's eyes lowered to his and when she spoke into the hush that had fallen over the room, her voice was quite unlike her usual cool, calm tone. It was almost guttural.

"Yes, I do. Their names are Meredith. Just like mine. What do you make of that, Inspector? And I'll save you the trouble of going on. Yes, I killed him, and you have no idea, no idea, how very easy it was."

Vivienne felt a pounding in her ears, as though the previous night's storm had invaded her body. She shrank further in her chair and shook her head. "It's not possible, Gina, tell them it's not true."

Alistair and Mali scurried over to her, both visibly shocked as they tried to comfort her.

Stevenson nodded to his sergeant, and she began to intone Gina's rights. "Ms Meredith, you do not have to say anything, but it may harm your defence if you do not mention when questioned something which you later rely on in court. Anything you do say may be given in evidence."

"Oh, I have plenty to say," hissed Gina. "I've kept quiet about what that bastard did to me for far too long. He raped me. I was fifteen. Fifteen." Her voice broke then and Vivienne got up, clearly wanting to comfort her friend.

"Sit down," Stevenson commanded so sharply that Vivienne quailed and fell back into her seat.

Gina's story came out in a rush, almost in one breath, as if she had held it inside for too long, coiled too tightly, buried too deep within, and now it was eager to burst free.

"My parents were Irish, staunch Catholics, and they inherited a farm in Lancashire, from some distant cousin. It was in the Ribble Valley, very picturesque as you know, Inspector. I was just a baby when we moved there. My parents were no farmers, though. The place was filthy and falling about round their ears, just a few chickens. My parents fancied themselves as artists and used one of the barns as a studio. They weren't interested in me, just in their art and each other. They never made any money out of it. It was a miserable place, cold, draughty, and so lonely and isolated. They tried running it as a B & B, taking lodgers, but no-one ever stayed long. It was too uncomfortable."

Gina took a shuddering breath now, seeming to steel herself for what was to come, her finger working at the hole in her jeans.

"He, Jeremy, came to stay the summer I was fifteen. Said he was working on a novel and wanted somewhere quiet to write. He didn't seem to mind the state of the place. It was cheap, I suppose. This was before he was successful. He was much older than me and he seemed so sophisticated. Told me all about Cambridge, the dinners, and his rooms in college. He said he couldn't wait to show it all to me. He told me he'd like to write about me, said he would put me in his novel. That I was his muse, his Northern Madonna. He teased me about my accent; it was stronger then. He read poetry to me. No-one had ever spoken to me like that. I thought… I thought…"

Gina's voice trailed away, her face fell forwards towards

her lap, and she raised trembling hands to her hair. When she lifted her head, her voice was steady, and her eyes had hardened.

"He was charming, funny, and clever, until he wasn't. He told me that he wanted me, he needed me, and he persuaded me, in the barn, while my parents were out. *Making love*, he called it, but there was nothing loving about it and afterwards he changed. When I talked about coming to see him in Cambridge, about our future, he laughed in my face. Said I was a country bumpkin and a whore, and he wouldn't be seen dead in public with me. He laughed at my clothes, at my hair, my taste in music. He said I'd been gagging for it, wandering around the farm in my tiny shorts. After that day, he came to my room every night and told me to keep quiet, or he would tell my parents what a whore I was. How I had pursued him. The things he did to me… I could never have told a soul. After he had gone, I realised I was pregnant. I couldn't tell my parents; they were anti-abortion. I was terrified that I would be stuck in that horrible place forever, tied by a baby. I couldn't trust my family GP not to tell my parents. I was under sixteen and it was 1985. I wrote to him at his publishers, to tell him about the baby, but he never replied. One of the girls in sixth form found me crying in the toilet at school and told me about a back street abortion clinic in Manchester that her cousin had been to. I used the money I'd been saving for university, from my Saturday job. It was awful, and the pain, the blood, afterwards…" Gina's voice trailed off and she shuddered, but again there was that hard flash in her eyes. "I have never been with a man since. I got out of there as soon as I could, vowed I would never be reliant on anyone, never wear the charity shop hand-me-downs my mother bought for me. I met Vivienne twenty years ago and being here has been the happiest time of my life. I finally felt safe. I could breathe. Then *he* turned up yesterday, just the same, arrogant, and full of himself. Look at all the lives he has ruined, people he has humiliated and abused. Still I wasn't sure what I would do when I saw him, how I would feel, but the way he looked at me when I showed him up to his room brought it back, everything I have hidden for so long. Then when I saw Mali coming out of his room with those pages last night, I had to know if he'd written anything about me, if he remembered, so I sneaked in to take a look. When I saw what he had written, I made up my mind. It was the utter contempt in his writing, you know. It brought it all back, all the shame, the humiliation. It was easy. I left the drawing room saying I was making coffee and slipped into the library. The light is dim in there, as you know, and he was by the desk, looking out of the window, when there was an enormous flash of lightning. It illuminated the room. He could see it was me. He was in a bit of a mess actually, his head already bleeding." A laugh passed Gina's lips, though there was no humour in it, only derision. "Do you know what he said to me? *Oh, it's you! Thank God!* He was relieved to see me, thanking God as if it were divine bloody intervention that I was there. Thought I would be his saviour." Another snort of laughter. "He deserved it, and I would do it again." Gina held her chin high, staring directly at the detective inspector, as if daring him to argue with her.

"I used that rat," Gina said, back to her usual brisk, business-like tone now, like she was tying up loose ends.

"You know," she nodded at her friend Vivienne. "That antique bronze paperweight. It's hideous, but very heavy, and it did the trick. I hit him twice to make sure. I hadn't thought there would be quite so much blood, so I took off my apron and wiped my hands and arms with it and used it to wrap the rat up. It's stashed in the bottom of the grandfather clock. I was going to retrieve it later, but it doesn't matter now. I cleaned myself up in the kitchen while the kettle was boiling," she finished casually, then something else occurred to her. "Do you know, I've just realised how fitting it was killing a stinking rodent like him with a rat." She giggled girlishly.

DS Ford cuffed Gina and led her out of the room. Police and ambulance sirens could be heard in the distance, but getting nearer every minute. *Thank God,* Ellie thought, *we can finally get out of here.*

CHAPTER 23

Everyone had watched in stunned disbelief as Gina, still defiant and chin jutting into the air, was handcuffed and walked out to the police van, whose sirens had announced its arrival and alerted them to the fact that the roads must have now been cleared.

Mali, Alistair, Oscar and Vivienne wandered trance-like back to the kitchen. Mali offered to make tea as Vivienne's hands were trembling so much.

Vivienne felt a heaviness descend on her, like grief. She was distraught that her friend, confidante and companion had been driven to such an act, and was mortified that Gina had been taken away. It seemed like a dream, a nightmare, the events of the day whirling around in her head.

As she sipped her chamomile tea, her despair turned to anger when her mind explored the story Gina had relayed, of the unimaginable abuse that she had experienced when so young, at Jeremy's hands. Gina had carried that torment for all these years. It distressed Vivienne to consider how it must have felt to be in her attacker's presence once again. She could understand why Gina had taken her opportunity to rid the world of such evil. She also understood now why Gina had been so adamant they book Jeremy as a guest author, in spite of her own reservations. Vivienne resolved to visit her friend as soon as she was able and let her know that she had her unwavering support.

Vivienne looked around this room that had always been so warm and alive with Gina's presence. It pained her to see the empty chair by the range; her half-finished book splayed across the arm. Her favourite coffee cup on the draining board made her heart ache. But it was the ugly pink vase on the windowsill that broke her. It was filled with roses, already dropping their petals. Gina said she had bought it herself with her first pay packet. She had always kept it filled with flowers from the garden. A tear slid down Vivienne's cheek as she considered how Gina had never had anyone to take care of her. She cleared up the petals and vowed to keep the vase filled for her friend's sake.

She glanced at the remaining guests, gathered in the kitchen. Dear Alistair, he had lost his sparkle, standing by the window drinking his strong black coffee and looking quite desolate. He threw her a sad smile, supportive as always.

Oscar too seemed to be reeling from the horror of the turn of events, his face drained of colour. He walked aimlessly around, stopped and came towards Vivienne as though he was going to utter some profound advice, then shook his head, turned and walked off in thought only to repeat this several times until Mali in her gentleness suggested he sit down with a nice cup of Ashwagandha tea to soothe his nerves.

Vivienne hoped that Mali might stay a while. She found her presence immensely comforting.

Harrison and Madeline lowered themselves in the cream leather seats of their Audi soft-top and closed the doors with more fervour than needed, as Harrison activated the central locking system; to lock them in. The silence enveloped them like a cashmere comfort cloak. Familiar scents, the car freshener, the blanket, and the leather, teased their nostrils and sent an overwhelming sense of home to both of them. Madeline pulled the blanket from the token back seat towards her and held it in her lap like a long-lost kitten. Harrison broke the silence first. "I'm sorry." She put her hand on his knee but couldn't look at him, for fear he might see how much what had happened had affected her.

"You don't ever have to apologise to me. I suggest we never discuss what happened here with anyone, ever."

Harrison mulled over what she was suggesting. A secret. A lifetime secret, of the most gigantic proportions. He knew he could trust Madeline with his life, but could he keep his mouth shut indefinitely? He never wanted to see this place ever again. Being here would remind him of it all. Just sitting there, he swore he could feel his ancestors breathing down his neck. He certainly didn't want to pursue any inheritance.

She hadn't taken her eyes off him, watching out for him. He may be a bit short in the old social/emotional understanding but one thing Harrison knew for certain was he had Madeline. Completely.

"Let's go home," he said. They both melted into the seats. He felt strangely guilty for being related to Jeremy, and for what the man had put Gina through all those years ago, causing a lifetime of suffering. Out of the two of them he was in Gina's lane.

Harrison adjusted the seat, mirrors, and heating. He set the accelerator, eased off the clutch, manoeuvred through a three-point turn and saw Ravenshade in the rearview mirror. He faltered for a moment, seeing the house shrouded cocooned in warm shades of autumnal splendour, sprinkled in pumpkin and spice textures. It was as if she was calling him back. The sun glinted in the mirror and made him blink, breaking the spell. He looked ahead to where the single-track country road would take them home, pushing the accelerator too hard, and causing the gravel to fly from the rear wheel spin as he sped down the drive. Harrison checked his mirror again but by then Ravenshade was smaller, less significant, the distance between them breaking the connection; but he didn't take his eyes from her until he turned the corner. Then Ravenshade was lost.

Pippa could hardly believe the events of the past few days. As she drove back to the university town, the familiar landscape rolling by her window, her thoughts turned to the whirlwind she had become part of: a group of strangers, each driven by their own motives, all converging on one enigmatic figure: Jeremy Pendleton, the once-renowned crime writer, now deceased. Murdered.

But most pressing in her mind was the discovery of the Codex, hidden for decades in the library, and as she had predicted on her arrival there to be found. Her head was alive with writing the article, and as she drove each sentence was written and rewritten again in her mind. The ancient manuscript would now be returned to the university library, where research into its origins and secrets could finally resume. The academic world would be abuzz. Pippa knew this was only the beginning of a remarkable chapter and one she was going to make sure she was included in.

The Eagle was lively that evening, its low beams and glowing fire offering a welcome warmth after weeks of long hours. Detective Inspector Dougie Stevenson sat with a pint of Coke in his hand, finally allowing himself to relax. Across from him, Detective Sergeant Ellie Ford was laughing at something the landlord had said before he moved on to serve another round of customers.

The pub was a regular for local coppers and a few of their colleagues propped up the bar. They too had reason to congratulate themselves and relax; a vicious burglar safely behind bars, the wreckage left by the storm largely dealt with, and no fatalities, in their county at least.

"Well, we cracked it, Ellie," Dougie said, lifting his glass. "Dead ends, red herrings, and eight suspects glaring at us across that draughty old dining room. But in the end the truth always comes out."

Ellie clinked her glass against his. "To the truth. And noticing the trivial things no-one else did. That misplaced bronze rat was the key, wasn't it?"

"Any one of them could have used it and then hidden it. I was pretty certain it was Gina though, as soon as I read that bit in Pendleton's diary about the Ribble Valley – her vowel sounds are pure Lancashire, just like my Granny's were. But Meredith couldn't bear the thought of her employer taking the blame for something that she'd done and I think she was desperate to confess," Dougie finished modestly.

"I couldn't help feeling sorry for what Gina went through. She was little more than a child when that monster came into her life." Ellie twisted the glass in her hand. For a moment silence hung between them. Then Ellie straightened, a hint of pride softening her expression, "Still, we did our job, sir."

Dougie met her gaze, a smile of satisfaction tugging at his lips, "We did. And tomorrow there will be another case, another puzzle. But tonight…" He pushed back his chair and stood, "we celebrate. Ready for another G & T, Sergeant?"

EPILOGUE

Despite her confession, Gina Meredith wanted her day in court and refused to plead guilty. Pippa championed her story and that of the thousands of women who are the victims of sexual violence and never get justice.

Detective Inspector Dougie Stevenson had earned his long-awaited break. He had retreated to the northernmost reaches of Scotland, where phone signal was patchy, and peace was practically guaranteed. No crimes, no suspects… nothing but the sea, the sky, and silence. Just how he liked it.

Back at Ravenshade Manor, Vivienne – once briefly under suspicion herself – had embraced her new role as the accidental matron of mystery. The manor is now a thriving hub of creativity, hosting sold-out writing retreats and niche workshops. The murder in her grand library, oddly enough, had turned into a marketing goldmine. Writers arrive in droves, drawn by the mix of inspiration and infamy.

Vivienne was the sole beneficiary of Jeremy's will; his

estate boosted somewhat by the brief resurgence in sales after the publicity surrounding his death. Vivienne wanted nothing to do with his money and used it to set up a charity supporting women who were the victims of domestic abuse. She visits Gina often.

Mali, ever content with the quiet life, returned to the soft hills of Wales with a sigh of relief. Her days are filled with tending to her herb garden, chatting with the locals in the village pub, and enjoying the kind of calm that only sheep and solitude can provide. Every so often, she finds her way back to Ravenshade Manor, not just to lead her beloved workshops on herbs and potions, but to slip back into the easy rhythm of friendship with Vivienne. Their evenings unfold slowly, filled with the clink of ice in gin and tonics, and the fragrant chatter of herbs, old remedies, and half-forgotten spells. Amid the laughter, scattered notes, and cluttered workbenches, something always takes shape: an idea; a tincture; a new path forward, proving that even in the heart of their beautiful chaos, there is always something worth holding onto.

Harrison and Madeline, despite their involvement in the less savoury parts of the case, walked away without conviction, and with a publishing deal. Their sensationalised, blood-soaked retelling of the three-day chaos became an overnight bestseller. They leave their agent to the book signings and tours, happy in their solitary life without complications.

Alistair, typically, disappeared on his own terms. Last seen heading to Peru, he left behind whispers of the Mayan Codex. Rumour has it he secretly photographed its pages before it was returned to Cambridge University Library. Nobody has heard from him since. Whether he has gone rogue or gone deeper into history, no-one quite knows.

Meanwhile, Pippa Whitcombe's columns on lost treasures and obscure artefacts have captivated readers across the UK and beyond. She is rarely seen without a notebook, always chasing the next story. She never confessed about Alistair photographing the Codex the night it was uncovered.

Oscar, the mature and respected art dealer, finally had his moment in the spotlight. His long-delayed exhibition opened to a full house at the Cambridge University gallery and was an instant success. Since then, he has become a fixture in the culture pages of the newspapers, always ready to unveil his next provocative curation. He stays connected with Pippa who, when she can spread the news on his exhibitions, always does.

And Ellie, the steadfast police sergeant who kept her cool through the storm, found something unexpected: love. She met Camilla not long after the case closed, and the two are now blissfully navigating a fresh romance. Ellie's set to become a detective inspector herself, on the force's fast track programme, and for once, she is smiling more than scowling, even though Camilla's family own a family seat in Northumberland and are one of the wealthiest landowners in the north-east.

In the end, Jeremy's tragic demise brought together a strange, brilliant, and sometimes bewildering group of individuals. The case is closed, but the stories live on, each of them changed, each of them with a tale to tell, and all of them knowing that sometimes the strangest chapters come after the last page.

One year to the day of the death of Jeremy Pendleton, the Mayan Codex that was being displayed at the Cambridge University Library was stolen for the second time. There were no signs of forced entry, no clear suspect, no explanation. Just a single piece of parchment left in its place and marked in red ink with the names of Vivienne Henderson, Harrison and Madeline Chester, Mali Pritchard, Alistair Fradley, Oscar Martin-Bramston and Pippa Whitcombe.

They were going to be drawn together again, this time into something far older, far darker, and far more dangerous than murder.

Meanwhile, Jeremy Pendleton's unfinished, unpublished memoir lay at the bottom of a box of evidence. On the last page of the manuscript, and preceded by many blank sheets, was an afterword he had long ago fixed upon as his valedictory close:

I know I am bound for a special place in Hell. All my adult life I have preyed on the weak and vulnerable and no penance, rosary or confessional will redeem what I have done. I have taken my revenge for the wrongs done to me. Remember this, all you who "suffer the little children to come unto you". Hurt them at your peril. One day they will grow up.

It is not known whether DI Stevenson ever read it.

The Write Word

Founders Jane Gill and Stella M. Ashbrook

The Write Word was formed to bring together like-minded, enthusiastic writers with a shared passion for storytelling and a desire to stretch their imaginations. From the start, Jane and Stella set out to create collaborative work that could also support charitable endeavours. Over the past year, each member—Anne, Jilly, Gill, Ann, Jenny, Helen, Julie, Jane, and Stella—has contributed their own distinct voice and character to the writing journey.

Their combined efforts have resulted in *Dying to Write*, a testament to creativity, teamwork, and determination. This publication marks the group's second collective achievement, and The Write Word is proud to share the outcome of their collaboration with readers, while continuing to champion both imagination and community spirit.

Julie

Ann

Anne

Jenny

Jilly

Gill

Helen

Acknowledgements

We have had so much fun writing this book and we have also had the opportunity to work with some wonderful people, who have been so generous with their time and expertise.

Firstly, local author, Kate Long who helped us to build characters and their backstory and set the best 'Revenge' writing task!

Secondly, Liz Hyder, who gave us such good advice about structuring a story and how to build tension. She was so positive about the whole project that it was infectious. Her mantra that 'everything can be fixed' when you are writing has been invaluable.

Finally, Katharine Smith of Heddon Publishing whose support with editing, formatting and printing has been indispensable.

Without their input, the end result would have been much poorer and the whole process much less fun. All the remaining mistakes are, of course, entirely our own.

Finally, Moo and Boom have provided us with tea, coffee and cakes each week – the lifeblood of all writers.

www.ingramcontent.com/pod-product-compliance
Lightning Source LLC
Chambersburg PA
CBHW032009180726
48283CB00008B/2603